THE
EVIDENCE
OF THINGS NOT SEEN

ISBN: 1-4392-4973-3
ISBN-13: 9781439249734

In loving memory of Carol Mastrapasqua who fought the good fight and is with God

CHAPTER 1

"Wake up, sir," said an insistent computerized voice. "Dr. McAllister, your presence is needed in the cockpit."

McAllister unzipped his sleep restraint cursing the computer under his breath. It was very difficult to sleep in the space shuttle's cuboid beds. Air jets kept a constant breeze flowing over the astronauts to prevent them from breathing accumulated carbon dioxide. The noise and cold generated by those jets made sleep hard to come by. McAllister was certain he had been asleep for only a few minutes. The computer chimed in with it's notice again.

"I hear you, computer; perseveration isn't necessary," he growled. "What time is it?"

"Ninth day, first month, year 2010," the mechanical voice replied.

"I know the date," McAllister griped. "What's the hour?"

"The elapsed mission time is fifty-six hours, ten minutes and twenty-three seconds."

"Predictable," McAllister grumbled as he floated through the living quarters. He had been asleep only a half hour, and the adrenaline rush from his rude awakening made him irritable as he crawled into the cockpit. He took a seat beside the pilot, Jim Neely.

"What have you got, Neely?" McAllister asked brusquely.

"An automatic laser warning," Neely said, his eyes glancing up. "It's your program; you tell me."

McAllister typed a query into the science station and read the screen silently. After a moment he flipped a switch and spoke to mission control. "Request permission to hold this orbital position. We have a finding I need to better define. Transmitting data now. Call in the ground team."

Neely leaned over McAllister's shoulder and whistled. "You're defining a space under the ice cap."

"A very big space," McAllister replied. "Near the foot of Mount Erebus. I need you to align *Adventure* with the South Pole and synchronize our orbit with that of the Earth. We're going to need to drill at least another three hundred sites to define our finding."

"We have to rendezvous with the space station at 1600 hours, sir," Neely protested.

"I'm certain you can obtain clearance to delay that rendezvous," McAllister said. "This is much more important than delivering parts on time."

Neely sat back and fought to contain his response to McAllister. He wanted to express the feelings of the entire crew regarding their scientist guest. Military decorum encouraged him to suppress his opinion. The task became more difficult when McAllister laughed triumphantly.

"Take a look at your screen, Neely. Proving one's hypothesis can be very gratifying."

Neely manipulated the space shuttle's controls. The scientist was brilliant, but McAllister had convinced the astronauts that he was an arrogant control freak. None of the astronauts considered his current research to be worthwhile, but they had been sufficiently repelled by McAllister's attitude to avoid knowing any more about the project than absolutely necessary. If they had overlooked their first impressions, they would have realized McAllister was earning a second Nobel Prize. They might have been excited by their role in the discovery.

In the eight days that followed, the crew did their duty and shunned the scientist during the off hours, which was exactly what McAllister had hoped they would do. His work was the scope of his life. He avoided any personal interactions unless absolutely necessary. He didn't really feel that decision had limited him. He had a career agenda marked by increasing successes, and he didn't want anything to interrupt those successes. He didn't believe in destiny, a God, or any part of his future being beyond his control.

He never felt empty or unfulfilled until he tried to sleep. He had read books on directing sleep and dreams, but he had never had much success. At night, his past haunted him. And so, he hated sleep.

Dr. Rachel Madison dismissed her eleven o'clock class on pictographic languages ten minutes early in order to attend the Archeology Symposia. It was a two-day meeting sponsored jointly by the Texas Research University and the Southwestern Museum of Antiquities. The keynote speaker and drawing card was Dr. Bryne McAllister who was discussing his latest book, *Tectonic Armageddon and Polar Shift*. Rachel was a linguist, but she belonged to both the archeology and language departments because of her work with ancient languages. She had loved archeology from childhood. She had been reading papers published by Dr. McAllister since her undergraduate days though she had not read his latest publication. She bought a copy in the foyer intending to use it as a reference during the lecture. Being seated on the front row was obviously an impediment to that intention.

Her choice seating was due to the number of people who had chosen to attend the lecture. The auditorium was standing room only when she arrived. Fire codes caused the lecture to be delayed for another fifteen minutes while everyone in the room was either seated or transferred to another hall to watch a televised version of the lecture. Rachel was given an empty front row seat because she was a tenured staff member.

As she walked down the crowded aisles, she attracted admiring glances from the male attendees. She had inherited her Mexican mother's curly dark brown hair and her father's iridescent brown eyes. It was an attractive combination. Her hair was in a pompadour that day with little ringlets loose around her face. Because she was the last person to take a seat, she caught the speaker's eye. She took his expression as disapproving and blushed in embarrassment.

McAllister had disapproved of the late arrival until he had seen her. It was as if she had an unseen aura irresistible to him. He had difficulty returning his focus to the task before him, and often during the lecture, his eyes moved to her as if of their own accord.

Rachel kept her eyes on her hands when she realized Dr. McAllister was looking at her. She felt as if everyone in the room would think she was flirting with the speaker. The thought of leaving the room was quickly banished as she became lost in the content of the lecture, almost against her will. Rachel was impressed with how dynamic a speaker McAllister was and how he was able to make her feel what it was to excavate worlds that had been vibrant and alive thousands of years earlier.

The direction of his talk was startling but well evidenced. He described well known civilizations and how climactic changes had abruptly contributed to their falls. This introduction led to a brief discussion of plate tectonics and then the concept of disasters prefaced by plate movement. He used the tragic Indian Ocean tsunami of 2005 as an example of minor plate movement. He then moved to a three-dimensional model of Pangaea, the united continental mass, and showed the potential effects of massive plate shifts.

"If continental drift occurred abruptly and not over millennia," McAllister theorized, "then an ancient, advanced society like Plato's Atlantis may be much further from the cradle of civilization than we have imagined."

He moved his computer presentation to a schematic of a laser drilling program. "The book's premise is a theory. This experiment is the beginning of the proof. This space is beneath the Antarctic ice cap and represents a very large area of previous unexplored ruins. This year, I will be taking a team to define these ruins and obtain the final proof that a massive continental shift has previously occurred and could occur again as a result of global warming."

Numerous questions followed that closing statement, and McAllister handled them effortlessly. Rachel found herself staring at him despite her intention not to make eye contact. It was difficult to imagine that he was anything less than completely correct in his assumptions. Only his refusal to use the abbreviations A.D. and B.C. made Rachel feel uncomfortable. A.D. stood for the Latin words *Anno Domini*, or "in the year of Our Lord." B.C. stood for the time before the birth of Christ. For two thousand years the world's time had been marked by the birth of Jesus Christ.

Secular archeologists and historians were seeking to change the nomenclature to B.C.E. or before Common Era and C.E. or Common Era. Rachel was repulsed by the action, and McAllister's use of the modern nomenclature made her surmise he had cast his lot with the nonbelievers. Still his words and his eyes drew her like a magnet.

As the lecture broke up, Rachel mulled over some questions to ask McAllister, but her thoughts were quickly cut short with a glance at her watch. To reach her next lecture she would need to leave now. As she walked down the crowded isles Rachel didn't see Dr. McAllister attempt to pursue her through the mash of students. He was defeated by the steady stream of admirers who surrounded him.

After a half hour of fielding more questions, McAllister was finally able to leave the lecture hall. The young student that caught his eye nowhere to be seen. The Archeology department's chairman, Dr. Neill Carson sidled up to him as they left.

"Masterful as always," Carson remarked.

"They were a receptive audience," McAllister replied. His response sounded rushed even to him, but at that moment, his focus was still distracted by the unknown woman who had mesmerized him. He struggled with how to work his quest for her identity into the conversation.

"I don't think you expected such a large audience, Neill. I was expecting the fire department would close us down before that last woman was seated. I know she was horrified to be escorted to the front row."

"I noticed," Carson remarked. "That was one of our younger instructors, Rachel Madison. She isn't the kind of woman who tries to draw attention to herself." Carson's voice revealed his admiration of that trait.

"How odd," McAllister said casually. "How does she sell her research proposals? Is she an archeologist?"

"Linguist," Carson replied. "She specializes in ancient pictographic languages so she belongs to both departments. She doesn't need to sell her ideas. She's very talented. She broke a primitive Chilean language that had baffled more than one expert in the field."

"When you see her, do offer my apologies," McAllister said. "I'm certain I deepened her embarrassment by looking her way while she was being seated. Do you know how many will be attending the lecture this evening?"

McAllister felt he had learned enough from Carson to undertake research on Rachel Madison privately, and he was successful in diverting the department chairman's attentions to the evening lecture. He was dragged through a number of social engagements for the remainder of the day, impatiently awaiting his chance to escape to the university library. Eventually, he made his excuses to the university hierarchy and left on the pretense of working out. He changed to jeans and an old soccer jersey and attracted no attention except when showing his British ID to gain admission to the library.

Once hunkered in a research cubicle McAllister accessed the computer file containing the curriculum vitas of the university staff. One look at her photograph confirmed the beauty on the front row was Rachel Madison. It was hard to take his eyes from her photograph and read the details of her professional life. The document told him that Rachel was an assistant professor in the departments of Language and Archeology. She was twenty-nine years old and had held her teaching position for three years. Her postdoctoral work was in ancient pictographic languages. She had published twelve papers, but her dissertation fascinated McAllister more than the others. It was a comparison of the linguistic similarities of pictographic languages in advanced North and South American cultures to the pictographs of Egypt and Babylon. As he read and reread the professional details of Rachel's life, an idea occurred to him. He never gave the ethics of the idea a second thought, which was also an action much out of character for him.

Rachel was shocked to receive a hand delivered invitation to Dr. McAllister's luncheon the following Monday. She knew he taught in the United Kingdom and expected he had returned to London after the symposium. When she called Dr. Carson, he informed her that Dr. McAllister had been working on a special project with ISC for the previous five months and was on a research sabbatical from the United British Universities.

"You should be honored to be invited, Rachel. You're the only one invited who isn't a field archeologist. He's proposing an expedition for this summer. I assume you may be invited to that as well."

"Why would he need a linguist?" Rachel asked. "Or does he expect to find hieroglyphs?" The thought excited her. She had never had the opportunity to be the first linguist at a dig. "Is this the dig in Antarctica?"

"If you want to know more, you'll have to attend, Rachel," Dr. Carson said somewhat irritably. It had occurred to him that McAllister might have ulterior motives in inviting Rachel, and if so, he wanted no part in it. Nonetheless, he knew it would be professional suicide to even suggest that possibility regarding an international guest.

"I'm quite sure Dr. McAllister will explain in detail. He did ask me to give you his apologies. He felt he embarrassed you when you were being seated before his lecture."

Rachel listened to Carson's voice over the phone and felt uneasy. She wondered if his tone and irritation was a warning, but she also knew she hadn't been able to stop thinking about Bryne McAllister since that day. She had studied up on the professor on the internet as well as the university intranets and as a result she found him to be even more fascinating. While good sense told her to decline the invitation, her sense of adventure bade her to accept.

Rachel was the last to arrive at the luncheon. She was startled by the small number of people at the table. She shunned the wine everyone else accepted and was sipping her water when she realized the guest speaker was smiling in her direction. She smiled back somewhat shyly and then gratefully turned her attention to Dr. Carson as he introduced Dr. McAllister. It was a time-consuming task. Bryne McAllister had a curriculum vitae that surpassed anyone in the room.

"Thank you for accepting my invitation," McAllister said as he took the podium. "You've all been invited here by virtue of your expertise. We share a passion in searching for the treasures of the past, and I know the data I'm about to show you will more than pique your curiosity."

He turned on his computer and dimmed the room's lights. While he was reiterating his preliminary data, Rachel recalled everything she knew about McAllister. He was forty-one and a British citizen who had been born in Wales and educated at Oxford University before its absorption into the huge United British University. He had several degrees listed including two doctorates. He had started his career as a geologist and had been awarded the Nobel Prize in science for his work in predicting tectonic plate instability using sonographic tracings interfaced with GPS positioning of the plates.

Recently, McAllister had been nominated a second time for his work with lasers. The weapons grade laser he had developed had the ability to penetrate ice, rock and sediment while causing minimal damage to any artifacts it encountered. It had allowed him to effortlessly map ruins from space. With a complex series of resistance measurements he designed, an investigator could easily determine the density of objects the laser encountered. Having read many of his papers, Rachel was familiar with the grids his work produced.

She scanned the first slide of his space shuttle data while trying to glance surreptitiously at McAllister. He had given her the impression of being tall, but was actually just shorter than Dr. Carson, who was six feet in height. McAllister appeared to be in good shape physically and had dressed in a tailored suit to flatter his physique. He was not wearing a tie, which made her believe he was a nonconformist by nature. His hair was reddish blond with a faint peppering of gray and he had a ruddy, outdoorsman's complexion with piercing blue eyes. He wasn't a strikingly handsome man, but he was attractive.

The surface photographs McAllister displayed were of an ice-covered landscape dotted with rocky peaks. She recognized it as Antarctica even before McAllister put a map of the continent on the split screen. As if he was reading her thoughts, McAllister brought his personal theories into the discussion.

"As we have all been involved in the search for advanced civilizations, we're familiar with the theories of the catastrophic events which might have produced the loss of a large land mass that might have housed something like Plato's Atlantis. The geological evidence documents that Antarctica was a part of Pangaea. I undertook laser drilling of the Antarctica land mass on a shuttle flight in January to search for evidence of early civilizations under the ice cap. We had already proven the accuracy of the laser technique on a prior shuttle flight by remeasuring known ruins.

"As you can see from this grid, I've localized a two-hundred square mile area of ruins near Mount Erebus on the edge of this frozen sea. The grid pattern from this area is striking and unexpected because of its variance, which suggests buildings, roads and a variety of building materials including dense metals. If the grid is correct, the Antarctic land mass could be Plato's Atlantis relocated to the South Pole by massive tectonic plate shift. A natural assumption would be that this occurred due to an asteroid strike. After seeing islands shift several feet just in response to a Richter nine seaquake, I don't think we can deny the possibility of a major continental shift," McAllister stated as he turned on the room lights.

"We've been constructing a dome with a self-sustaining generator system that will allow us to continue digging through the winter safely. So that we can reach the station before the winter storms begin, we will need to leave in the next few weeks. I've obtained permission to stage the team from the military installation near Deception Cove. If you choose to participate in this project, your current salaries will be continued through your institutions, and you'll receive a stipend equal to a year's salary."

Rachel glanced at the other attendees. There were six men, some of whom had brought their wives or significant others. She knew the partners wouldn't be invited to the actual dig and wondered if she should risk being the only woman among so many men. She was involved with an Air Force pilot and could not help but wonder what his reaction would be if she chose to go.

McAllister consulted his list and began a roll call. "Dr. Carson?"

"Count me in," Carson replied.

Rachel knew the department chairman's acceptance of the offer represented an even greater incentive to the other academicians present. She made her decision long before her name was called. Everyone present accepted McAllister's offer, and later

Rachel wondered if any of them had really understood what an undertaking it would be.

McAllister gave each of them an envelope as they took their leave. It was then that Rachel was formally introduced to him. Dr. Carson did the honors.

"Of course, you know Dr. Madison on paper, but allow me to introduce you. Dr. Rachel Madison, this is Dr. Bryne McAllister."

McAllister took her hand like any other colleague might have, but his hand felt different to Rachel. A surprising warmth seemed to connect them. Rachel felt almost breathless as she looked up at the world famous scientist. She didn't know she was having the same effect on him.

"I'm honored to be invited to the dig," she stammered.

"Your work has certainly earned you the right," Dr. McAllister said. He hoped his voice didn't sound unsteady and hurried his next comments. "I will be needing your input. If we're right, you may be very busy translating."

"I'll be ready." She stepped back as if repelled by how he made her feel. "If you'll excuse me, I have classes this afternoon." She nodded to Dr. Carson and took her leave without seeing Bryne McAllister's eyes follow her from the room.

In her car, Rachel examined the papers and found a list of equipment she would need and a rough draft of their itinerary. She had fifteen days to be ready to leave for five months. On the way back to the university she alternated between celebrating and having second thoughts. Beneath her uncertainty was a sense of exhilaration. She drove to her father's house before going home. He was the one person she dreaded telling.

Andrew Madison was a colonel in the Air Force who had been assigned to the space agency for past twenty years. He had risen to the position of director of the astronaut program with the International Space Consortium in 2005. Her father had been a pilot and an astronaut, but had grounded himself after a near fatal crash. The decision had held his family together when his wife, Isabel, had died from a cerebral hemorrhage less than a year later. Rachel had been a freshman in high school when she lost her mother. Her older sister, Nicole, had been a junior.

Colonel Madison had raised his daughters alone seeing them through the heartaches and joys of high school and college. Nicole had obtained a degree in early childhood education. After teaching for three years, she had married a ISC civilian engineer, Steven Tanner. They had a two-year-old son named Richard.

Rachel had attended the Texas Research University for college and graduate school. She had returned to Houston permanently after two years at digs in Mexico and South America. During her absence, Colonel Madison had married a base widow named Emily Morton. Rachel liked her stepmother and was happy for her father because she knew the unpleasant side of being alone. She had also known a measure of resentment because her father and sister had a sense of belonging she believed she might not ever find. Even as she walked toward her father's house, Rachel wondered if he would notice her absence if she didn't tell him of her impending departure. He startled her when he met her at the door.

"I was hoping you would come, Rachel. Are you sure this is the right thing to do?" Her father's anxious brown eyes told Rachel he would have noticed and cared more than she wanted to admit at that moment.

"How did you know?" she asked casually.

"McAllister has permission to use space at the naval base in Antarctica," Colonel Madison said. "He sent a computer list of his team to the Naval authorities this afternoon. I have friends in all branches after so many years in the service." He sat down on the sofa and patted the space beside him. "I know you're old enough to make your own decisions, Rachel, but you've never signed on for anything this dangerous. What does Gary think?"

"I haven't told him yet, Dad, but I don't think he'll really care. He's a pilot through and through. He has his life, and I have my life. When we have the chance to be together, that's enough for him. I don't think he looks beyond the next mission he'll be flying. I'm not sure I want to live with that kind of uncertainty forever. I do know I don't need to commit when I'm not absolutely sure."

"You're right," the colonel conceded. He thought Gary was a good choice to become Rachel's husband, but Andrew Madison wasn't a controlling parent. He wanted his daughters to be as happy as he had been with their mother. "I have the station plans, and I think you'll be safe enough. I guess this expedition just seems a lot like going into space. Trying to rescue you during the Antarctic winter would be almost impossible. Once you're there, you'll be there until the spring thaw."

"I don't think Antarctica sees much of a thaw," Rachel said as she smiled. "I've always said I could give up television. Now I'll have to prove my claim. I have a year's worth of reading to do. It's not like you're giving me a cyanide capsule just in case something goes wrong." It was a reference to a fact only an astronaut's family would know. In the early days of space flight, no one had known if the astronaut pilots would make it home. Rescue missions hadn't been an option. An emergency kit had always been given in case of the unexpected.

"I'm not expecting any problems, Rachel. I'm just not looking forward to going so long without seeing you," Colonel Madison said gruffly. "Even when you were in the Andes, you didn't seem as far from home as you'll be this time. I'm making arrangements for a special piece of equipment. Leave some room in a suitcase. When do you have to leave?"

"In two weeks. Dr. McAllister seems to be intensely organized." She scanned her father's face. "What do you know about him?" Her expression made her father nervous because it told him she was interested in McAllister. The scientist's reputation made Rachel's father against that interest. He made a strong effort to discourage it.

"He's not the boy next door, Rachel. Both shuttle crews had issues with him, and the last crew was a bunch of low key, easy going guys. According to them, he's cocky, arrogant and self absorbed. You know he's an atheist?"

"I didn't, but I'm not surprised. Maybe that's why I'm supposed to go," Rachel said. She leaned forward and hugged her father impulsively. "I'll be all right, Daddy. After all, I have a black belt."

"I'm not worried about your ability to defend yourself physically," he said. "McAllister is a brilliant man. The powers at ISC think he's the next Stephen Hawking. They like him because he

12

knows how to get a job done, and he doesn't let anything get in his way. Some of the astronauts probably didn't like him because he memorized the shuttle flight manual during basic training. He knew enough to fly her after two months of training. Unfortunately he didn't seem to know enough about people to keep that knowledge to himself."

"Is he working with ISC on this dig?" Rachel asked. "Why would ISC be interested in ancient ruins?"

"We're silent partners. These ruins might be from an advanced civilization. There may be metals in the ruins we don't have. It could be an amazing experience being there for the discoveries, which is why I didn't have the heart to ask you not to go. I've always felt guilty about keeping you from your first love." He sighed. "Just be careful." He returned her embrace and said a prayer that God would keep her safe when he couldn't. Then he made plans to talk to her boyfriend on a need to know basis.

In a Houston bar, Neill Carson stood to greet Bryne McAllister. "I was beginning to wonder who diverted you from our meeting."

"If I'd had a better offer, I might have left you in the lurch," Bryne replied. Actually, he hadn't seen anyone socially in years, but he didn't want Carson to know how much he hoped to change that fact. He chose his drink in an effort to relax the tension he was feeling. "Neat scotch." The waitress smiled in response and disappeared into the depths of the bar.

"I expect you've been ready to leave for weeks," Carson remarked. "Do you think the team will be ready on schedule?"

"I looked at their prior dig performance before considering them," Bryne said. "Everyone who signed on has a history of punctuality."

"I haven't heard that anyone is having problems making ready," Carson conceded. "Between the two of us, I'm curious as to why you asked Dr. Madison to come. She is a talented linguist, but you could have chosen an archeologist with linguistic experience or another geologist. You don't even know if you'll need her expertise."

"She's very qualified, and we certainly won't have the option of sending for other members if we find we need them." Bryne answered glibly to keep Carson from seeing how deep the current of his interest in Rachel ran. "Even if we don't find translation work for her, she's aesthetically pleasing."

Dr. Carson had long courted Bryne McAllister to get him involved with his department, and he knew his next words could permanently damage their relationship. He spoke because he could not let the implication of an ethical breech pass.

"If you're expecting to look and not touch, she'll be an asset no matter what the outcome, Bryne," Carson said. "I can tell you now that she's not going to be with us for your pleasure. She isn't that type of woman."

"Perhaps you don't know her or me as well as you think," Bryne retorted. "Care to make a wager?" Carson's intrusion into his personal thoughts goaded Bryne into doing something extremely out of character. "A hundred dollars says I'll have the lovely Dr. Madison completely in my sway within the next month."

"I don't gamble on people's lives," Carson protested. "I should probably warn Rachel that you have ulterior motives for asking her to join the team."

"If you made that sort of accusation, you'd have no way to prove it," Bryne snapped. "Dr. Madison is qualified and agreed to come. Whatever might happen on the dig will happen between consenting adults."

An uncomfortable silence fell between the two men. Carson knew he had pushed as far as he dared. Though his own background was well established, he was certain the university might sacrifice him to appease an angry demigod. He finished his drink and stood. "If I intend to be ready on your schedule, I'd best be tying up my loose ends. Let me know if I need to make any other arrangements."

Bryne nodded curtly and turned his attention to his food as Carson left the bar. He had the feeling that Carson would inform Rachel of their conversation. He was sure his chances of a relationship would be ended if Carson did portray him in that light.

As he agonized over a salvage maneuver, he tried to call the one friend who would understand and encountered her answering machine. Then he couldn't bear to leave the bar for his empty apartment and continued drinking to keep his place there. He was in no condition to drive home at midnight. The waitress volunteered to take him, and the encounter that followed was not a judgment call. He regretted it from the moment he awakened beside a stranger. He had no idea of the impact the encounter would have on his future.

CHAPTER 2

His team was a week from departure when Bryne fell ill. Normally stoic, he felt sick enough to fear his upcoming isolation from medical care. A viral DNA/RNA probe rapidly confirmed that Bryne was infected with Cytomegalovirus, strain 16. CMV-16 was known to be sexually or blood acquired and couldn't be prevented by the usual "safe sex" measures. It ran a six to eight week course that involved rash, fever, low-grade hepatitis and very often a mild encephalitis. It was linked to the almost eradicated demyelinating diseases of the 1990's.

"Antiviral drugs will generally protect you from complications, but you should probably postpone your immediate travel plans," the doctor advised him.

"That isn't an option," Bryne said tersely. "We have a very narrow window of opportunity. What alternatives do I have?"

"You'll have to assume the risks I can't predict if you choose to go. I can put you on an anti-viral cocktail. You can take a monitor and transmit blood test results to me weekly so I can tell you how you're progressing." He drew up an injection and used a laser spray device to deliver the dose. "You might want to limit your sexual activity with strangers, Dr. McAllister. The people who carry this disease might give you something we can't treat. You're very lucky this is the only virus you have now."

Bryne was still horrified by his own indiscretion, but he hid his response under a show of macho bravado. "I appreciate your concern, but you're assuming a great deal." He stood slowly because of his aching joints and collected the prescriptions the doctor had written. Then he went home to brood.

McAllister needed someone to listen to him vent that night, but there wasn't anyone. Even the friend he had tried to call would not have understood how he had made such a stupid mistake, and he didn't want her to see him in that light. He was glad she was en route to join the team and couldn't be reached because he felt weak enough to confess his sins despite that consideration. He saw his illness as a final and insurmountable barrier to a relationship with Rachel Madison, and he tried to convince himself that it might be for the best. He had grown up in state custodial care, and those years had reinforced his belief that emotions were often used against people foolish enough to display them. He had only become emotionally involved once in his life, and he had never recovered from that relationship.

The tangible symbol of his lost love was waiting for him when he sat down in his bedroom. He could almost hear her laughter. Bryne couldn't forget how she had made him feel as if every moment of life was precious. When he looked at her picture, he felt sick. He put the photograph face down on the nightstand. The laughing eyes made him think of Rachel Madison again. He ached to have the feeling of being content with life once more. That void in his life was responsible for a much deeper ache than the ache of his illness.

He was drawn into the maelstrom of his memories that night and the two days that followed. Relief didn't come until the anti viral therapy took effect and restored fifty percent of his usual energy. He fled his apartment as soon as he felt well enough to dress.

"I'm definitely not optimal but I'm unquestionably better than I was," Bryne informed his physician. "How long will it take until I'm no longer contagious?"

"Four weeks is the average," the doctor admitted reluctantly. He suspected that McAllister was looking forward to exposing himself to other sexually transmitted diseases. "I'll be able to tell from your blood work. You should have my transmission data and the blood extraction devices by now. Make certain you send me a sample weekly. Keep in mind, this virus is lethal in a small number of people."

"I've studied the layman's information," Bryne said. "Let me know when I'm no longer a risk."

McAllister drove to the Texas Research University that afternoon and slipped into the lecture Rachel was giving. He had hoped to find a seat on the front row, but the room was filled to capacity. It was her final lecture to her class in basic Hebrew. She was preparing the class for the final examination by writing passages on the board and assisting them in the translation. McAllister had to stand at the back of the room, and he would have been willing to stand and watch Rachel for much longer than an hour.

"I don't think this can be talking about taking the city bus," she laughed. "This is an ancient Hebrew course, Mr. Hernandez. I hope you've been here often enough to know that."

The class laughed, and Bryne McAllister found himself smiling almost involuntarily. He couldn't take his eyes off Rachel as she moved from the right side of the board to the left, quickly translating the passage.

"Go into all the world and preach the gospel to every creature," she said. "Despite Mr. Hernandez's little joke, I'm certain you're all ready. You might want to review tenses tonight." She bowed to them and said, "Shalom."

Bryne found himself smiling like the young male students who obviously admired Rachel on many levels. He couldn't ever remember being on such a personal level of communication with his students. She seemed to enjoy the contact. Bryne remained in his seat and watched her with interest until the last of her students had departed. She was cleaning the board when Bryne moved to the front row and cleared his throat to get her attention.

"Good afternoon, Dr. Madison."

"Oh," Rachel said. "You surprised me, Dr. McAllister. I thought everyone had gone."

"I was hoping to be on the front row as you were for my lecture," he said. "You had a capacity crowd. After seeing you in action, I would imagine all your classes are filled to capacity."

"Not all of them," she said. She continued cleaning the board to avoid his gaze. His gaze made her feel flattered and uncomfortable at the same time. She didn't want to let her eyes be drawn to him when he would see she felt powerless to look away.

"This class is always full. There's a divinity school here in Houston. All the students in it want to learn ancient Hebrew and Greek so they can work out their own ideas about what the Bible says."

"You speak Hebrew very well."

"Do you speak it?" Rachel asked curiously.

"Enough to order deli in Jerusalem." He thought his words might sound arrogant and added, "I've been on digs in that area of the world. I know you must be wondering why I'm here. I'm trying to get to know all the team members on a more personal basis as we'll be spending five months together. May I take you to lunch?"

The suggestion seemed harmless enough, and Rachel nodded. "If you could give me a moment to finish up here, I'd be glad to join you."

"I have a car just outside," he said. "I'll pull round to the front door."

He was driving an expensive sports car which didn't surprise her. He got out to open the door for her which was unusual. His attire bespoke his wealth. He was wearing an open collared white shirt and gray silk suit. She wondered how he had managed to garner a fortune as a teacher and researcher.

"I thought you lived in London," Rachel said to break the awkward silence.

"London is my home base, but I travel a great deal," he said with relief. "I suppose travel is an archeologist's worst occupational hazard. I've been tenured at the United British University for the last six years. I came to Houston five months ago to work on the laser project with ISC. I gather you've lived here for a long time."

"For half my life. My father is with ISC."

"Colonel Madison. I know him from my work there."

"I heard you flew on the shuttle," Rachel said. "Did they waiver the astronaut training for you or did you get the works?"

"The works," Bryne reassured her. "I doubt that your father would have waivered them if I had had the nerve to ask. It was quite an experience. I was particularly fond of the microgravity simulation. Have you ever tried it?"

"I've flown planes," she said. "I wanted my father to let me try the 'vomit comet,' but he considers it to be solely a training maneuver."

"How was it growing up as an astronaut's daughter?"

"Unnerving at times. I think it made me into a dare devil when I was younger." She was impressed that he had passed the astronaut's training program without asking for any special favors.

"I can't see you as a dare devil," he said as he drove into the parking lot of Houston's most expensive restaurant. "What experiences allow you to claim that title?"

"I climbed mountains, learned to scuba dive and went kayaking down level five rapids. My dad used to call me 'no guts, no glory.'"

"I've always liked that sort of adventure myself," Bryne said. He stopped the car and gave his keys to the valet. Then he hurried to help Rachel from the car. His hand on her arm made her want to be even closer to him.

She felt as if she was being unfaithful to Gary, but entering the restaurant pushed that thought from her mind. She had never been there, and she was appalled by the prices of both sides of the menu. McAllister seemed very much at ease with the price and the place. Ultimately, she asked him to order for both of them.

"Do you come here often?" she asked as the first course was delivered.

"Actually no," he said. "I tend to grab a salad or sandwich while I'm working. Do you come here often?"

"Oh, of course," Rachel said. "My salary and this restaurant are completely compatible." McAllister laughed.

"It might be that I'm trying to impress you. I could have taken you to a pub, but I noticed you didn't have any wine when you came to the luncheon."

"I drink water, tea, coffee, milk and juice. I don't imbibe." Rachel was smiling against her will.

"Probably no one should," he conceded. "In Europe, it's almost cultural to have wine or alcohol with your meal. Of course, in some restaurants it's probably the only reason one can survive the meal. I have the impression that you're very religious."

"I'm a Christian," Rachel said. "I gather you aren't."

"You shouldn't assume," he said. "Everyone has me pegged as an atheist. I'm really more of an agnostic. I take the scientific approach. I'm waiting for proof."

"I don't think God wants us to find proof," Rachel said boldly. "The Bible says faith is the substance of things hoped for and the evidence of things not seen. Most of the scientific theories that try to explain the creation are accepted without definitive proof."

He was surprised by her logic, and his face expressed his reaction. "I haven't ever heard that particular theory. You're saying you believe God has deliberately concealed the evidence of his actions in the past?"

"I do," Rachel said. "The Bible says He showed Himself to the people and worked miracles before their eyes. With irrefutable proof before them, some still doubted Him. Now we have to trust and believe. To ask God to prove He exists is like asking for someone to prove that they love you.

"I have to say that I don't believe in agnosticism," she continued. "Either you believe in God or you don't. You gave your opinion away when you used the nomenclature, B.C.E. and C.E. instead of B.C. and A.D in your lecture."

"That doesn't necessarily reflect on my beliefs," Bryne said hurriedly. The conversation had taken on a painful sense of déjà vu. "That nomenclature is standard at our university now. We have an ethnically and religiously diverse faculty, and some of them take religious offense at the B.C. and A.D. nomenclature. It was quite difficult for me to comply with the university's request at first."

Rachel felt relieved at the explanation, and the feeling showed in her face. "I'm glad to know why. We also have a diverse faculty, but I won't compromise what I believe. I'd have to resign if the university asked me for that concession." She studied his face seeking answers to unspoken questions. "Am I going to be the only person of my faith on the seventh continent?"

"It's considered politically incorrect to ask such things when you interview potential team members, but I know there will be at least one other Christian with us. Her name is Melea Adams.

She's quite an expert on Plato and a splendid linguist in her own right. I would think you might enjoy the opportunity to persuade the unbelievers. You seem to be quite effective at arguing your point."

"I didn't think we were arguing," Rachel said somewhat defensively.

"I don't see arguing in the same light," he said quickly. "To me it's just a sharing of ideas like debating. You seem well versed in a great many subjects." He paused as the waiter served the second course and struggled with how to change the subject.

"Why did you call these ruins a possible Atlantis?" she asked. "I've done some reading, and if you believe Plato, it should be in the Atlantic."

"I don't know if it's Atlantis," he responded with relief. "I don't necessarily believe there was a civilization called Atlantis. By the time Plato wrote his descriptions, it was a legend. There are extensive ruins in Antarctica. Irregardless of who lived there, they're very ancient based on their depth. If you belief in continental drift, we're discussing millennia. However, I suspect something catastrophic may have shifted them abruptly at one time, and I'm not alone in my belief.

"I'm an archeologist for the sake of convenience most of the time," McAllister chuckled. "My actual agenda is to prove massive tectonic plate shift has happened once before and could happen again if there are great changes in the polar ice caps from global warming. I'm rather like Noah's ark in my team selection because I don't know what we'll find. We're taking an ancient animal archeologist, an ancient plant archeologist, a linguist and field archeologists with ancient Egyptian experience. Now tell me what you believe."

"I'm a linguist," Rachel said, "but I believe in the idea of an astral body striking the ocean floor off the coast in Puerto Rico in 8500 B.C. and flooding the coastal land bodies. I hadn't ever heard of polar shift until your lecture." He looked amused, which made her feel irritated. "What makes you think this dig will confirm that?"

"It's a possibility we'll confirm the theory. Then again we may just find out the entire earth was once a jungle. I see in your eyes that you think I'm quite a fanatic. Have you read Leonard Shelby's book?"

"I haven't heard of him," Rachel said. "I've just started reading your latest book."

"Leonard is a geologist who's very devoted to the idea of polar shift. I'll have a copy sent to you."

"Before you waste your money, you should teach me about what plates and continental drift and polar shift are. I haven't studied geology since high school."

"Well, no scientist should ever stop learning especially when they teach. You could become stagnant." He took her hand. "Lecture one in plate tectonics. Make a fist. That will be our earth's core." He put his hands around hers as if they were a shell. His hands were warm as they caressed her fist.

"You have the crust, the mantle and the core. My mantle is touching your core, but it can still move and shift to accommodate the changes in the core beneath it because of the space between them. Simplistically, my hands are the tectonic plates that lie beneath the dirt under our feet. They rest on a cooler plasticene layer of the lower mantle called the asthenosphere. The plates are composed of the outer mantle and crust that makes up the lithosphere. They're like pieces of a spherical jigsaw puzzle. They have the ability to move around quite a bit. Where they touch are the fault lines. There are all sorts of faults, depending on how various plates move with the other plates around them. Continental drift is the idea that all the continents were once a part of a giant land mass. As new mantle and crust are formed on the sea floor, the land masses are pushed farther apart.

"In your scenario," McAllister continued, his hands still cupped about Rachel's, "the asteroid displaced the plates in the ocean and caused a sudden, simultaneous shift of all the plates. As a result, a large piece of Pangaea breaks off and lands at the South Pole. Polar shift is the idea that the ice caps might have melted enough to change the pressure on the poles. That could cause all the plates to move at once. What was up might then move down quite abruptly." He released her hand reluctantly and met her gaze hoping to see acceptance of more than his theories.

Rachel couldn't keep him from seeing her admiration. He was an excellent teacher. The more they talked, the more she felt drawn to him. There was a complete absence of arrogance in their private conversation. Even Bryne's motives for the dig were more humanitarian than she had assumed. She had always devoted a portion of her free time to ecological causes, and his battle against global warming appealed to her.

There were no further awkward moments. The time seemed to pass too quickly for Rachel. When they finished lunch, she expected to be driven back to the university. Instead Dr. McAllister said, "In the interest of knowing you better, I'd like you to show me your favorite place in Houston."

"Get on the interstate," she said. "Drive toward Galveston."

"Galveston? You'll have to direct me. I haven't ventured out of Houston often."

"Could you put the top down?" she asked. He seemed happy to comply.

It took forty-five minutes to reach the beach at Galveston bay. Rachel directed Bryne to a parking lot adjoining a walkway. The sun was brilliant overhead, and the water was lapping over the white sands.

"This is my favorite place," Rachel said simply. She slipped off her sandals and got out of the car. Dr. McAllister took off his own shoes and left his suit coat on the car seat as he followed her down the beach. Rachel's hair blew in the breeze and made the team leader want to touch it. He walked more quickly to catch her and then walked beside her in the wet sand.

"Do you like the beach?" she asked.

"I didn't for a long time," he said. "I had some unpleasant childhood memories of the sea. Then I learned to dive in order to participate in an underwater excavation. I fell in love with the silent beauty of the ocean. It's very like space in that way."

"I love diving, but my dream was to go into space," she confided. "Dad asked me not to do it. It was the only thing he ever asked me not to do so I had to listen. Archeology was my second great love."

"So you settled for second best?" he asked.

"I believe all things are directed by God," she said simply. "There's some reason why I'm meant to do what I do. That's not second best. That's God pointing my way, but then you don't believe that's possible

"What you call divine direction, I've always called luck, fate and destiny, not that I believe in any of those things either. I'm a scientist, though. I keep an open mind on all fronts. What are your dreams now, Dr. Madison?"

"I don't really know," she said as she turned her face into the wind. "I always thought I'd teach until I got married, and then I'd be a wife and mother. At the same time, I've found myself wanting to do more as an archeologist. I suppose God will point me down the next road just as He always has. What do you dream of doing?" She smiled. "I can't imagine what you dream about when you've already done what people dream of doing."

"I've spent all my time on my research so I suppose I'm still waiting for my final destiny as well. It's a bit sad to admit such a thing at my age, but of late, I've realized that I do want more than academic laurels." He took a paper from his pocket with kinship driven bravado and gave it to her. "Can you translate that?"

"Is this a test?" she asked as she took the paper.

"If you like." His expression was as cryptic as his answer.

The glyphs were a contrived message about a joining between Isis and Osiris. They were the Egyptian goddess of eternal life and god of the underworld. Mythology said they had been married. Rachel assumed the message was intended to arrange a sexual liaison between them. She flushed as she returned the paper to him.

"I don't think you found that on a temple wall."

"It was intended as a social invitation." His face was suddenly serious. He was sure he had offended her, and it had been very unintentional. "Keep in mind that ancient languages aren't my field. I meant to suggest we could see each other socially if you were interested. I'd really like to get to know you outside of our professional relationship." His words were almost pleading and kept Rachel from answering immediately.

"I can't," she said as she tried to gauge his sincerity. "I'm in already in a relationship." She felt a rush of uncertainty as she spoke the words.

"How unfortunate for me," he said. He hoped his emotional response wasn't as visible on his face as it was in his gut. "I suppose I'll have to settle for your company in the workplace."

"That isn't why you asked me to be a member of the expedition, is it?" Rachel asked.

"It wouldn't be ethical for me to mix my personal and professional roles." He resumed conversation as if she hadn't just turned him down.

In the car, Rachel felt she might have been too brusque in her refusal. She had a distinct impression that Dr. McAllister's eccentric note was a facade to protect himself from rejection. His eyes seemed to convey much more than disappointment when he left her at the university. After they parted company, she couldn't stop thinking about his eyes.

Bryne was devastated by Rachel's refusal. He only got through it by telling himself he would have time to make her share his intense attraction during their sojourn in Antarctica. Then his ethics told him that further pursuit wouldn't be right. Rachel had made her position clear. As he packed his belongings for the expedition, he became progressively more depressed by his inability to shut her out of his mind. Wanting to escape the magnetic pull she had on him fueled his decision to leave for Argentina the next morning.

The team was scheduled to travel on a charter flight to Argentina. Bryne left three days ahead of them and took a hotel room on the docks overlooking the boat that would take them to Antarctica. What he didn't take with him, he shipped back to London. He left Houston planning to never return to the city again, but before leaving he ordered Leonard Shelby's book for Rachel and had it delivered to her home.

When the book arrived, Rachel expected to find some sort of message from the team leader accompanying it. She was unexpectedly disappointed to find it was simply a book wrapped in plain brown paper by someone working at a bookstore. Holding it in her hands Rachel allowed herself to realize how attracted she was to him despite major differences between them. The memory of his attentions was empowered by Gary's reaction to her decision to go on the dig.

Rachel had explained Gary she was going on a field assignment as a preface to the whole story. He had shown no interest in her plans or even in when she would be returning. Feeling insulted and rejected, she had decided to tell him nothing more. Gary learned the full story from Rachel's father and immediately asserted an injured lover's indignance.

"You didn't say that your field assignment was in Antarctica," he said as Rachel opened the door.

"I didn't hear you ask," Rachel said. She held the door only slightly open until Gary forced his way into her home. The gesture was more threatening than comforting. At that moment, Rachel had the fervent desire to show him he wasn't her only option.

"It's a little late to argue," Rachel said as she closed the door behind him. "I'm leaving at ten tomorrow."

"What if I ask you not to go?" Gary said. His eyes were riveting, and Rachel couldn't avoid his gaze. He was flawlessly handsome, but somehow he no longer seemed attractive to her. She sat down on the sofa.

"Why now?" she demanded. "Do you realize what an opportunity this is for me? If we find what we expect to find, I'll be able to name my position at any department on the planet. I've never interfered with your career even when it kept us apart."

"Maybe that was different," he said. "Maybe we weren't so close then."

"Are we close?" Rachel asked. "This doesn't make me feel close, Gary. I don't feel like you'd be asking this now if you weren't trying to keep me from being around other unmarried men. For a long time I've been waiting for you to decide where we're going with our relationship. You've never said a word or even intimated that we have anything beyond this moment. Finally I started praying to know what to do, and I decided if you didn't ask me to stay that would be my answer." The uncertainty in his eyes spoke before his words.

"I just wanted to be sure, Rachel. I know you believe marriage is forever, and I don't want to make a mistake."

"Gary, I'll be back in a few months. Maybe time apart will give you your answer. See other people while I'm gone, and if we're meant to be together, you'll know." It hurt to see his relief. Rachel realized she had wanted him to beg her to stay and not to accept a negative answer. After three years of dating, she knew they both should know. Not knowing meant their relationship was just convenient.

"If that's what you want, you'll be shutting my feelings out of your life," he said defiantly. "The rumor mill says you're going to be running from Bryne McAllister for the next five months. When I see how much you want to go, I have to wonder if you're looking forward to the prospect."

She felt as if he had slapped her face. "You need to leave, Gary," she said. "If you don't, we might destroy everything we've had with what we say next."

He looked shocked, but he nodded slowly. When he told her goodbye, she had the impression that this goodbye was forever. Everything about the encounter told her that Gary didn't love her even though she didn't want to accept it. She felt terribly alone then and took out the sheet containing the names and addresses of the other team members. She dialed Bryne McAllister's number expecting he would answer and needing to hear his voice. A recording told her to leave any urgent messages with the United British University as the number had been disconnected. It took a long time for Rachel to sleep that night.

CHAPTER 3

Rachel was about to call a cab when her father arrived the next morning. He was in uniform, and it occurred to her that he was facing their separation as if she were going on a mission. Before he carried her bags to the car, he placed a plain brown box inside one.

"It's a satellite seeking transmitter," he said simply. "Covert teams carry them into hostile territory. We have communication satellites passing over the South Pole several times a day. If there isn't one of ours in range, it will lock onto anything above you and deflect to a friendly device. I'll have a remote receiver with me all the time. This is the frequency."

"Can I get it through customs, Daddy? I'll bet I'm not supposed to have it."

Rachel hardly heard him answer because she was remembering watching him walk into the space shuttle twenty years earlier. She remembered sitting in her mother's lap and praying he wouldn't die in an unknown place so many miles from home. Colonel Madison hadn't changed much in appearance despite those years. His wavy dark brown hair was as free from gray as her own. He was sixty but the years didn't really show in his appearance. As she looked at him, Rachel remembered how many years he had spent as a solo parent to Nicole and her. He was a good man and the kind of man she had wanted to marry. For the first time, she was feeling she might not ever meet a man like her father, and the thought made her sad. Her father seemed to read her thoughts.

"Gary doesn't want you to go, Rachel. He told me he wanted you to stay."

"He's jealous," she said simply. "I don't think he has a higher motive. I don't think he really wants forever. I'm not sure he ever will. I'd expect us to know after all this time so maybe we need distance to know." Rachel put her arms around her father. "I'm all right, Daddy. This is like you going into space. It's something I'm supposed to do. I asked God to give me a sign, and how Gary acted was a sign."

The answer made Arthur Madison feel a father's anger. He had a nagging impression that Gary had been stringing Rachel along in hopes of helping his career, but he didn't want the failed relationship to send his daughter into an even worse relationship.

"Don't go on this journey expecting to find your soul mate, Rachel. I've heard Bryne McAllister intends to pursue you for reasons we won't mention. He has wealth, power and intellect, but his reputation says he's everything you don't want in a husband."

"I knew to be wary after our first meeting, and I'm perfectly capable of holding him at bay. He's awe-inspiringly brilliant. I'm sure I'll learn a lot from him." She zipped up her duffel bag. "Time to go."

"The radio is broken down to make it through customs," the colonel said. "Use it every day if you have time. I'm really going to miss you."

"It's just five months," Rachel said fighting back her own tears. She felt as if she were abandoning her best friend and counselor. "Take care of yourself, Dad."

She locked her door while her father loaded the car and then gave him a set of keys and instructions about watering her plants. In the plane, watching her father wave goodbye, she cried. Her depression deepened when she realized the team leader was not on the plane. She had wanted to see him.

The pilot was unknowingly merciful, and their time at the gate was short. She didn't even have time to greet the other team members, although she noticed the decidedly feminine hat near the front. In the air, Rachel was overwhelmed by her sleepless night and slept until the flight attendant awakened her for lunch.

"Long night?" the flight attendant asked.

"Just wondering what I'm doing here," Rachel said. "Two women and seven men on a glacier for five months. I must be nuts."

"You'll have your choice of how to keep warm," the attendant teased. She put a tray and a bottled water in front of Rachel. "Eat up. You'll get a sandwich before we land, and that's it."

"Archeologists don't usually have the luxury of being decadent," Rachel said.

The food was good, and she was hungry. When the trays were taken, the other female team member came to meet her. Rachel knew her name was Melea Adams and that she was a full professor of Archeology at Princeton University. When Dr. Adams sat beside her, all of Rachel's other imaginings about the older woman were quickly swept away. Dr. Adams stuck out her hand as a man would have.

"I guess we'll be rooming together. I'm relieved. I thought I might be the only woman on the dig. I'm Melea Adams." She had a raspy, alto voice and the freckled face of a red head who hadn't ever shunned the sun. Her hair was so streaked with gray that it appeared frosted. Wisps of it were escaping from a series of braided coils.

"I'm Rachel Madison. Dr. McAllister told me you're the leading international expert on Plato and Atlantis."

"Bryne has a tendency to exaggerate," she said. "I'm just another archeologist looking for something that might not exist and enjoying every minute of the search. I haven't been on a field assignment in a very long time, but I couldn't turn this one down."

"I haven't been on a dig in three years," Rachel said. "What do you think we're going to find? You don't sound like you think we're going to find Atlantis."

"We're going to find something ancient and history altering," Melea said. "I'm not expecting to find Atlantis. For all we know, Atlantis was a legend. I do believe there was an advanced civilization before the Egyptians and the Greeks. I understand your major research is in pictographic languages. How much have you read on the theories of Atlantis?"

"Very little," Rachel admitted. "I've only just started with Plato's accounts. I bought copies of *Timaeus* and *Critias* in the original

Greek," Rachel said. "I hadn't ever heard of Dr. McAllister's explanation for why the advanced civilization disappeared."

"We had all assumed it was a catastrophic local event like a volcanic eruption. If Bryne is correct, Atlantis was probably just a legend to the Greeks, and the true scope of what the Atlantians had may have been lost with time.

"Have you seen the hieroglyphics in Egypt that suggest helicopters, airplanes and space crafts?" Melea asked. "I've seen them, and to see them is to believe there might have been a civilization on this planet that was more advanced than our own. I don't know what these ruins are, but the dimensions are intriguing. It must have been big, and the new sonographic data looks like there are refined metals in the ruins. They're already using an oil drilling rig to create a shaft down to the center of the ruins."

"Does Dr. McAllister believe it's Atlantis?" Rachel's attention was abruptly redirected from her own musings by Melea's expression.

"Bryne is a muse. Life is more of a multiple choice test than a short answer examination to him. I think he believes our civilization followed another even more advanced civilization that was destroyed by massive continental shift. Since he's a geologist and a very good one, I have to listen to him when he says polar shift is a real possibility. It's actually a worrisome idea because global warming could trigger it again. It's the thought that loss of polar ice mass causes the poles to be lighter in mass than the other continents. That might trigger all of the tectonic plates to shift to stabilize the mass balance. North America could be where Argentina is. Mexico might become the South Pole. Flooding would destroy everything coastal.

"Clearly there was worldwide flooding at least one point in time," Melea continued, "because there are submerged ruins off shore of most every continent. We know a human kindred coexisted with the dinosaurs so why did we live so many millennia without advancing and then come to this level in a mere seven thousand years? It would also explain the remnants of advanced knowledge the Egyptians, Mayans, Incans and Anasazi people shared. They might have been the survivor races. They had the knowledge but not the technology. All the legends were the same. Maybe Orion's fall from the stars was the fall of a people reaching toward the stars."

She laughed at Rachel's expression. "Yes, I'm as impassioned as Dr. McAllister. My late husband was my role model and Bryne's mentor. He was a very free thinking Egyptologist. It's a risk being a free thinker. You might wind up with a Nobel Prize. You could be considered mad as a hatter for the rest of your career." Melea shrugged.

"So, you're primarily a linguist?" she continued after a moment. "Neill Carson was filling me in on the details of the team. I gather you were a late addition."

"Dr. McAllister apparently spoke with Neill about needing a linguist," Rachel said uncertainly. "I only met him a few weeks ago. He seemed very certain that my skills will be needed."

"A part of believing in Atlantis is believing there was a root culture and a root language. My husband, Arthur, and I lived in Egypt six months out of the year. He was working on the excavation under the Sphinx. I'm sure you know some scholars believe it's ten thousand or more years old. In 1997, we spent an entire year there. It was our last dig together. Some ancient writings have suggested there's a library containing all the knowledge in the universe beneath the Sphinx, but no one has ever been able to get into the chambers under it. We made a heroic effort that year.

"We pumped out as much ground water as we could, and then my husband and his team entered the space in wet suits and tanks. They found a chamber filled with glyphs like the ones in the temple at Luxor. They showed clear evidence of airborne vehicles. They made photographs and documented that chamber for a week. Then they moved into the next chamber praying to find the library. We were in radio contact with them, though the water and the thickness of the rock made that contact tenuous. They simply disappeared. We never found their bodies or any traces of them. The search went on for nine days. We were forced to stop when two of the chambers collapsed."

"No one knows what happened to them?" Rachel said in horror.

"They died," Melea said matter-of-factly. "Something catastrophic happened. So many of the Egyptian ruins were booby trapped. I've prayed it was fast. I still have nightmares of watching them drown or suffocate." She stared at her wedding ring as she turned it on her finger. "I couldn't go on any digs for a long time. This is my first real dig since then. I suppose it means something to be going from one of the hottest spots on the planet to the coldest spot on the planet."

After a long moment she smiled weakly. "I think I'll just move my gear over here and get to know you better."

It was a ten-hour flight, and they arrived well after dusk. Rachel didn't notice the time after Dr. Adams came to sit beside her. Melea was fifty-nine, and she knew everything about the men on the plane. Rachel had only known Neill Carson until that day. Carson was one of her department chairmen. He was an Egyptologist but had spent nine years in Pompeii and on Crete including a stint doing underwater excavations off the coast of Crete searching for Atlantis. He had written two books on the ancient literature pointing toward a real civilization named Atlantis rather than a hoax perpetrated by Plato. He was married with two grown children, but he traveled extensively on digs. His reputation was as impeccable.

The second oldest man was James Tolliver who was fifty-three. He was a tenured professor at Harvard and had extensive experience categorizing fossilized plant life. During the previous year, he had been on sabbatical at the Texas Research University. He was divorced for the fifth time, but his reputation as a ladies man had waned. Like Carson, he seemed a stabilizing factor for the mission.

Armand Marquette was a physical archeologist. He had coauthored Leonard Shelby's treatise on the polar shift theory and as Shelby's partner, he carried information on the theory no one else in the world had seen. He was gay and had a reputation for risqué behavior, but Melea knew him to be a good scientist who kept his personal life distinctly separate from his professional life. He was tenured at the Paris Archeological Institute.

Raymond Gibar was a Russian who had immigrated to the United States. He had twenty years experience in digs in Siberia and the Arctic Circle. He had categorized plant and animal life there and had experience extracting and analyzing ancient DNA from insects inside amber. He was a director at the Smithsonian Institution. He was also married to a Smithsonian biologist and seemed to be devoted to his wife and his work. He was forty-seven.

The fifth man was Georges Christobal, an Austrian who had worked among the Roman ruins scattered through Europe. In doing that work, he had discovered a buried Roman archive referring to Atlantis. The work gave more details regarding the island state, and Christobal had made four trips to the Mediterranean searching for the lost civilization. He had contacted McAllister two years earlier, and they had corresponded extensively. Melea knew nothing of his personal life except that he was single.

The sixth man was a computer expert who had accompanied several of the university's expeditions and recorded the data. He had signed on reluctantly because his wife was expecting their second child. The stipend promise had sealed his destiny because he was not yet tenured. His name was Mason Farmer, and Melea felt he would be with them only as an extension of their equipment. His heart was obviously elsewhere during the flight. He nodded to her only once as he took a break by walking the aisles. He was short, small boned and had thick dark framed glasses.

"Why didn't Dr. McAllister come with us?" Rachel asked at the next lull. She found herself hoping for a more personal glimpse of the team leader.

"Bryne is meticulous in his planning," Melea said frankly. "I expect he went ahead of us to attend to last minute details. His life is devoted solely to his academic and research goals. He's a full professor at UBU and has been since he was thirty-five, which just doesn't happen there. Normally people are paying their dues well into their forties. The university funds whatever he suggests because he always comes up with something big. This laser technique will probably net him a second Nobel. When you consider his background, his success is all the more amazing." Rachel's eyes asked the question, and Melea continued.

"His father was a Welch coal miner. He died in a cave in when Bryne was seven. Bryne had two younger sisters. Apparently his mother cracked under the pressure and shot her children and then herself six months after her husband's death. Bryne lived through it. He grew up in government custody and earned every academic honor that could be had in the UK. He went to Oxford on full scholarship at the tender age of sixteen, graduated summa cum laude at nineteen and then earned two postdoctoral degrees before he was thirty. One is in geology and physical science. The other is in archeology. He has at least enough hours for a doctorate in physics in what he did to develop the laser program."

"He's never been married?" She regretted asking the question almost immediately because of Melea's expression.

"No. Supposedly, he has an active social life with a number of women, but I find that unlikely. He's never been a social butterfly." She looked at Rachel curiously. "Is your interest more than professional?"

"No," Rachel replied slowly. It was difficult to hide her emotional reaction to Bryne's life story, but her father's warning kept her distanced from her desire. "I was just curious. He never mentioned anything outside of the expedition when we've spoken."

"It's easier that way," Melea said. "It's probably better not to mix business and pleasure."

"Anyway, I'm already involved with someone else," Rachel said defensively. "I've been seeing an air force pilot for the last three years." She hesitated. "I'll admit to being attracted to Dr. McAllister when we first met, but he gave me a message in hieroglyphics that made me feel like I was being picked up in an Egyptian bar. I don't think he's looking for a permanent relationship." She was embarrassed and didn't see the sudden flicker on Melea's face.

"The one certain thing about Bryne is he's never dull. He has an odd sense of humor, and I suspect you were a victim of that. I've never known him to be crass or vulgar, and I think he would like to have a permanent relationship if the right woman came into his life." She gave Rachel time to make further comment, and when it didn't come, she sat back in her seat.

"I think I'll have a nap. We'll be landing in an hour. I'm sure Bryne will meet us there." Melea pulled a mask over her eyes and leaned her seat back. Rachel followed suit but felt irritated when she closed her eyes and saw Bryne McAllister's face. She could say she wasn't interested in him, but her mind kept betraying her.

Bryne loaded his gear on the ship late in the afternoon on May fifteenth. It was a cold late fall day in Argentina, and an icy wind seemed to be bringing Antarctica to him as he stood on the docks. It was the first day he had felt physically ready to undertake the expedition. Early that morning his doctor had responded to his blood transmission with the message that his counts were trending toward normal values.

Bryne pocketed the two pill bottles before leaving his cabin to meet the charter flight because he knew they were crucial to his ability to complete the dig. He had purchased triple the amount needed because of that fact and packed the extra in his luggage. He was still afraid the open bottles might be taken or accidentally discarded if he left them unattended.

He met his team as they left the jet way shaking hands with each of the men. It was an effort not to go straight to Rachel. He put his arm around Melea who responded in kind. Rachel was surprised and taken aback because their behavior told her they were very good friends rather than simply colleagues.

"Dr. Adams, it's a pleasure as always," Bryne said. "Did you pack your insulated underwear?"

"Wanting to borrow them, Bryne?" Melea countered. "I'm so pleased to see you that I might be persuaded to share. I wondered where you were when I got on the plane in Houston."

"I was compelled to make certain everything was ready." He gestured toward a van. "Let's take a ride down to the docks." He moved to Rachel's side and reached for her bags. "It's good to see you again, Dr. Madison." The instant attraction she felt for him was almost frightening.

"Thank you," she said. "Don't worry about my bags. I'm nicely balanced." She regretted the comment before it had cleared her lips.

"So I've noticed," Bryne said. He gave her a wicked grin and moved away to lead the team to the waiting van. She smiled in spite of her intention not to respond.

They reached the dock at midnight local time. A downpour greeted them, and they were all soaked before they had their gear on the ship. A purser led them to their cabins. It was only the beginning of the hardships they would face that night. There wasn't any warm water on board, and the wall heater in their cabin was slow to warm the room. Rachel put on three layers of clothes and wrapped herself in the bedclothes. She sat shivering for two hours and wondering why she had come in response to what was probably an illicit invitation. She was feeling angry and resentful when a knock resounded at her door.

Bryne extended a thermos to her across the blast of cold air. "I thought the two of you might need this until the heaters get warmed up. It's hot tea."

"Thank you," Rachel said hesitantly. Even with his kindness, she was driven to question him regarding his motives in inviting her to be a part of the expedition before it was too late to turn back. At the same moment, she was so attracted to him that she couldn't think of how to proceed so she plunged ahead without any consideration for how her questions would sound.

"Since the day we had lunch, I've been told you had ulterior motives in choosing me for your team, Dr. McAllister. I feel like I have to ask you if it's true before I'm committed to months of contact with an unscrupulous leader." His face revealed his horrified response in color and expression.

"May I come inside to give my answer?" he asked tersely. "I'm very cold, too, and you do have a chaperone."

Rachel stepped back to admit McAllister and glanced at Melea's bunk. Her roommate was already asleep despite the cold. McAllister closed the door but stayed beside it.

"I weighed many factors, Dr. Madison, but I think most in your favor was your dissertation. I wanted a linguist who had already looked at ancient languages as being derived from a single root language. If this is a mother civilization, the translations of their writings will be critical. I hope that's an acceptable reason."

"I've been told I might be here as a potential conquest, and after the message you gave me at lunch I thought that might be true."

"If that had been my goal, Dr. Madison, I wouldn't have used hieroglyphs to ask you," he replied. "I'm forty-one years old so I believe I understand some of the nuances of asking a lady out. I genuinely wanted to see you socially, and if my attempt was gauche,

I plead a lack of experience in dating my colleagues. You've made your position quite clear so I've moved on with my life despite your rejection. I'm here to look for the ruins under the ice cap. What you will or won't do on your private time is really of no concern to me as long as you get your work done. If you can't work on my team, have the professionalism to tell me now and I'll have the captain put the gangplank out."

Rachel was embarrassed and intimidated by Bryne's brusque response. It suggested that her attraction to him had become one-sided. Self preservation told her to go home. Career considerations bade her to stay.

"I just needed to know," she said. "I'm a professional. I wanted to know if you were. I'll see you in the morning."

"Good night then," McAllister replied. He was frustrated and irritated as he walked back to his cabin. He was also disappointed in her response because his intense attraction to Rachel had not waned at all. He had wanted to believe the way she made him feel could be mutual. His frustration was intensified when he walked into the cabin he shared with Neill Carson.

"Getting your face slapped, were you?" Carson asked.

"I'll call off the bet right now," McAllister retorted. "You were quite right. She isn't that kind of girl." He dropped the money on Carson's bed and went to the bridge to watch the ship set sail. He was tempted to disembark.

CHAPTER 4

When she was finally warm, Rachel plugged in her computer and went onto the Internet. For the next two hours she pulled up information on Bryne McAllister. His credentials were understated on his CV. He had published over a hundred papers and three books. As she had read before, his first Nobel Prize was from the development of an ultrasonic technique to measure tectonic plate movement potential. The technique had perfected the ability to predict earthquakes and volcanic eruptions long before they occurred. He had developed the technology when he was twenty-five. It was in worldwide use and was credited with saving millions of lives.

The computer record confirmed his doctorates were in geology and archeology. He had more than double the hours necessary for a doctorate degree in physics and enough hours for a masters in higher mathematics. There was no mention of a personal life except that he was an internationally recognized soccer player who had played on the UK's Olympic team twenty years earlier. Remembering Melea's story about his childhood, Rachel moved back thirty-four years and scanned the archived newspapers in Wales for the McAllister name and then for the name Bryne McAllister. What she found colored her thinking about the team leader forever.

Murder/Suicide in Liston   *Wales October 31, 1975*

Joan Easton McAllister, age twenty-seven, was found dead from a gunshot wound to her head early this morning after her young son staggered into a rural farmhouse. Seven-year-old Bryne McAllister was critically wounded by a bullet to his chest but managed to walk five miles to get help. He is currently in stable condition at St. Vincent's Hospital. Also found dead in the car were three-year-old Margaret McAllister and five-year-old Leah McAllister. Both were killed by single gunshots through their hearts.

Mrs. McAllister was widowed six months ago, and her friends and neighbors reported she had been very despondent. None of the neighbors voiced any suspicion that she would be capable of such a heinous crime. An open Bible was found on the car seat beside her.

Rachel had always had the ability to envision what she read. She formed a very clear picture of the injured little boy staggering alone in the dark over five miles of macadam roads. She was crying when she turned off her computer. She was certain Bryne McAllister was scarred horribly from the experience even if he had managed to hide those scars. She was also certain the event was responsible for his feelings about God. She prayed for Bryne McAllister for a long time before she could sleep. She felt the ship set sail and wondered if the rough sea would make her sick. Instead the rocking helped her put aside her cares for the rest of the night.

Melea awakened at five in the morning. She was certain her roommate had been up very late and moved very quietly to avoid awakening Rachel. She went to the mess hall and was surprised to find Bryne was already there drinking coffee and staring at an open book. Since she had heard his conversation with Rachel the previous night, she was well aware of why he looked so tense.

"Have you been up all night?" Melea asked. "As I recall, you only have coffee when you haven't slept."

"I wasn't tired, and I had things to do," he said. "Look, Mum, how I'm feeling isn't something you can remedy. I've made a mistake in selecting my team, and it's something I'll have to live with for the next five months."

"You regret inviting Rachel Madison," Melea said as she sat down with her own coffee. He looked at her sharply.

"I do hope you weren't eavesdropping last night," he said.

"You've never been all that difficult for me to read, Bryne. It's clear that you're attracted to her, and since you've never mentioned her to me, I knew she was a spur of the moment addition to the dig. I sat with her on the plane. She's lovely. You have good taste."

"I was swept off my feet from the moment I saw her," he said softly. "A most unfortunate circumstance since the attraction must go both ways. She's given me no sign that she fancies me. Since you've spent time with her, what would you say my chances are?"

"About the same as a snowball's chance in hell," Melea said flatly.

"Thank you so very much," Bryne retorted. "Have I told you how I revere your optimism?"

"She tells me she's been involved with an Air Force officer for several years, Bryne. I have to admit that she seems quite interested in you beyond the scope of the dig, but I don't think she's interested in a superficial relationship."

"Why is it that everyone assumes that's what I'm seeking?" He knew the answer. The reputation he had cultivated to isolate himself was now condemning him to unwanted isolation.

"You've let everyone believe you're completely superficial," Melea said. "I didn't tell her why I know that isn't the case."

"Silence can be golden," he said darkly. "Where are we going with this, Mum? I like Rachel very much, and the feeling was completely unexpected. I never expected to feel anything for a woman after losing Arielle. I looked down from a lecture podium, and there she was. I couldn't take my eyes off her face. I haven't been able to clear my head since then. It's rather like being a gangling school boy. I'm developing a great respect for tales of unrequited love. Shortly I may take up reading the Austin sisters' works."

"I think the lady may be protesting too much," Melea said coyly. "She was very, very curious to know more about the professional and personal aspects of your life." Bryne eyed Melea skeptically.

"I'm almost afraid to ask, but as usual you're in charge of this conversation." He smiled faintly. "What do you think I can do to better my chances of success?"

"Undo the notion that you're some sort of sex-starved cad. The note gave her a decidedly bad impression."

"I asked Arielle out with a note like that one," Bryne said. "She responded in hieroglyphics. I suppose it was an error borne of nostalgia."

"Arielle didn't have everyone else telling her what a bad boy you are. You'll have at least four months to charm Dr. Madison. Brooding is not charming." She felt success when he smiled.

"You're a human antidepressant, Mum. As you'll be rooming with Dr. Madison, please promote my cause."

"I will because I love you. I would like you to consider that maybe God's playing a role here, Bryne. Sometimes He pushes people into doing what they should." She saw he was not convinced and took his hand. "Come with me please."

He followed her without question and walked to the windows overlooking the approaching port. "What is it you want to show me?"

"Deception Cove," Melea replied. "It was once used it as a harbor. Then sailors discovered it's the caldera of a volcano."

"You are speaking to a geologist, you know?" Bryne said.

"I'm not speaking to you on a scientific level, Bryne Jacob. It's a curious thought, isn't it? You can have all that snow and ice around a volcano when the water can be as hot as Satan's fireplace."

"The sort of place where a snowball might survive the heat." Bryne kissed Melea's hair. "All right, Mum. I'll have another go at it. Just help me in any way you can."

A loud bell rang to awaken the passengers. Rachel was surprised to see the ship was docking at the Antarctica military base. She hadn't believed the boat would be capable of such speed. She was warmly dressed except for her face, and after two minutes she returned to the cabin and put a transparent veil over her face to seal in the warmth of her breath. Dr. Carson joined her at the railing. He was similarly attired.

"This is a balmy day for the south pole," he informed Rachel. "It's only twenty-five below zero. Outside the dome mid winter it will get to 150 below or lower."

"I'm well aware of the weather we'll face," Rachel said tartly. "I brought everything I'll need to stay warm."

"I wish I could say I had. I'm already missing my wife." He diverted his gaze and then continued, "Watch out for McAllister, Rachel. His interest in you goes beyond this dig."

"I'll be all right, Neill," Rachel said firmly. "I grew up on military bases. I have extensive experience in dealing with wolves."

"You'll need it," Carson said grimly. "Don't underestimate how ruthless he is. He does whatever will advance his cause."

"Everyone does to some degree," Rachel said. "Let's just focus on the dig, and if we all focus in that direction maybe we'll keep him focused on it."

She left him because she was tired of conversations about McAllister's motives. Other than giving her the hieroglyphic note, the team leader had been less aggressive in his advances than other men she had known. She felt guilty for having been so quick to judge him based on other people's opinions. As their ship docked, she walked around the deck, keeping her distance from the other team members. The landscape was very foreign, the world of an ice desert. At the far horizon the beach was dotted with seals and penguins.

"It's really quite lovely in a stark way," Bryne remarked from behind her. "Not so pretty as the beach at Galveston but still striking." His voice was warm and not nearly as intimidating as it had been the previous night. His face was also covered with transparent veiling tucked into a navy blue parka. The color of the parka made his eyes look even more brilliantly blue.

"You know it's a desert of sorts," he said. "You'll see a myriad storms this winter, but there's not much precipitation. The winds just blow the ice particles around."

"How often have you been here?" Rachel asked.

"Twice before," he said. "I came before I went on the shuttle to have a mental picture of the terrain. I came back to map the area I mapped in space just before I summoned the team. I've not been here in the winter, and I have to say I've wondered at my sanity for choosing this time of year to dig."

"Why did you choose the winter?"

"Two reasons." He leaned against the railing. "The first was access to the drilling equipment. It's used for oil drilling in the other seasons. The company operates off the coast of Argentina, and the weather at sea can be so bad that they close down for the winter. The second reason is to avoid intruders. This could be a very big discovery. If we find what we expect to find, next summer this could be a dangerous place what with looters and other less scrupulous archeologists."

"You're very sure of our success."

"I'm very sure." McAllister smiled. "I have a reputation of being rather cavalier in the defense of my theories. That's rubbish really. I'm quite calculating in selecting the risks I take."

"I don't think you understand how that sounds," Rachel commented. "I think of calculating in a very dishonorable connotation."

"In some circles it is. In the academic world, careful evaluation of the odds for success is essential to your career. You must be fairly certain of success before you start asking people to give you their money to prove your ideas. Everytime you fail, you're less likely to be funded again.

"I'm glad you chose to come, Dr. Madison. I think you'll be pleased when you see the results." He put a hand on her shoulder simply as a gesture of camaraderie. Rachel moved away involuntarily because his touch conveyed a magnetic pull between them. McAllister stepped back immediately, overcome with embarrassment.

"I should have carried your bags off the boat last night," he said. "I don't expect you to like me, but I do expect your respect as a colleague. Frankly I don't know if I can tolerate your behavior for the duration of the dig. If you still want to leave, I'll pay your way."

He left so quickly that Rachel scarcely had time to process his response much less react to it. Then she flushed with shame. She had never been guilty of prejudice, but she was still judging Bryne McAllister by his actions. She fled to her cabin as a sanctuary until the sailors came to off load her baggage. In her cabin she knew McAllister's touch had been completely innocent. She thought she should apologize and knew she couldn't find the words. She spent an hour trying not to call her father for advice before going to join the rest of the scientists to ride to the military base.

Rachel and Melea were assigned to quarters on an opposite end of the base from the male members of the team. There were ten female officers and enlisted soldiers stationed on the base, and they were sharing the area those women called home. As soon as she had showered and changed, Rachel was summoned to the commander's office.

"Dr. Madison reporting as ordered, sir," she said to the naval Commander.

"Good morning, Dr. Madison. You're being afforded an unusual courtesy because of your father's long service to the government. You have a message from him and from Captain Gary Loftis. I thought you might want to use the screen to communicate. I made them both aware you would be available at 1100 hours." He gestured toward his com station and bowed slightly as he left the room.

Rachel said, "Thank you, sir," and moved to take the commander's chair. She expected to see her father's face when she turned on the screen and was startled when Gary appeared.

"Hi," she said uncertainly. "I was expecting Dad."

"I know," Gary said. "Rachel, I had to apologize. I've been really stupid. And scared of committing. I know I should have come to a decision before now, but sometimes I guess shock value clears your head. I tried to make it to your house before you left yesterday, but I got stuck behind a transport accident so I hope you'll forgive me for asking this now. I don't think we need to see other people. I know what I want. I want to marry you as soon as you get home. I hope you'll say yes." He studied her face through the screen as if searching for the answer he expected and wanted. "I love you, Rachel." Later, the words would seem almost like an afterthought.

"I love you," she said and felt it was a sign of what she should do. "Do you want me to come back now?" She wanted to believe that the pause that followed was not his real answer so she focused on the words.

"I'd like to fly down and get you, but it wouldn't be right. You're committed to this project, and if you leave now your professional reputation will be ruined. You've sat in Houston waiting for me more times than I want to remember so I'll wait for you this time.

I'm interviewing for a civilian job at ISC so we wouldn't have to be separated again."

"Are you sure, Gary? Are you really absolutely sure?" Rachel said.

"I'm totally and completely sure. I just need to hear you say yes. I've asked your dad and he said 'you took your sweet time, Captain.' I hope you're not quite as ticked off as he was, Rachel. If you'll forgive me for being a total idiot this time, I promise I won't ever be this much of an idiot again."

"I want to marry you," she said firmly. "I wish I could hold onto you and tell you, but if you'll meet me in Argentina in about five months I'll make up for lost time." His smile made her warm.

"I'll be there, and I'll be on line every night at ten PM, Houston time. Figure out what that is in Antarctica, and we'll have a standing date."

"I'll be there. I love you, Gary. I feel a whole lot better now. I felt like I wasn't ever going to see you again."

"That couldn't happen," he said simply. "I can't live without you." The transmission ended abruptly, and Rachel couldn't call the screen up again. Moments later, the commander reentered his office.

"I'm sorry. I know you lost your connection. You're about to get an official winter welcome to the South Pole. There's a big storm blowing up, and it plays havoc with our transmissions. You might want to go get some lunch and then Dr. McAllister wants to meet with everyone at 1200 hours. If I get another message from either of them, I'll send for you."

"Thank you, sir," Rachel said. "It was very nice of you to give me this privilege." She floated through the hallways hearing the howling winds but feeling untouched by everything around her. It was the aura anyone feels when they've finally realized a dream. She went through the mess line with the other team members and sat down with Melea. Her only moment of discomfort was when Bryne McAllister took a seat near her. He made absolutely no eye contact. The five months ahead of her no longer held any excitement.

Three thousand miles away, Gary slid into a booth across from Jon Burton, his navigator. "How did it go with Rachel?" Jon greeted him.

"She said yes," Gary said with no small measure of pride. "She didn't even hesitate."

"Well, good show," Jon said. "You're a lucky man. She's gorgeous and smart. When's the big day?" He was startled when Gary shrugged.

"I don't know. I don't even know if there will be a big day. I was just tired of being taunted by every fly boy at ISC because she's spending the next five months with Bryne McAllister. If Rachel is engaged to me, I won't have to worry about Dr. Nobel Laureate wooing her at the South Pole. Meanwhile, I intend to make sure she's the one, and there's no better way to do that than seeing other people. I've got us both fixed up for tonight."

"You know, I don't think her father will be really happy with you if he gets wind of what you're doing," Jon said uncomfortably.

"I've been doing it for a long time," Gary grinned. "Nobody has a clue. Least of all Rachel and I don't really feel guilty about it. I've been seeing her for three years, and she's still hard line about no sex until we get married. That's a longer dry spell than any man could live with." He waved at the two women standing at the door. "I guarantee you these ladies are very easy to get to know."

CHAPTER 5

The storm isolated the Antarctica base for three days. The station was even cut off from the Internet and all other satellite transmissions for the last two. Rachel had a feeling that this was going to be commonplace.

"Reception is always bad here," the commander explained. "Even in the summer, the cloud cover can block the signals. It's almost like a natural damping field."

That night the radar showed the storm passing, and Bryne gathered the team to make plans for their departure the next morning. "They'll be taking us by crawlers. Because we have so much equipment, we'll require four vehicles total. The dome is thirty-seven miles from here, and the trip will take ten hours. Be ready to leave at seven o'clock. You might want to contact home tonight because we won't know how the transmissions will be from Erebus base until we arrive." He stood and left the room leaving no time for questions.

Melea followed him and caught his arm in the corridor. "I had wondered if you were still here."

"I've been marinating myself in a bottle of scotch," he said acidly. "I've seen no chances for the snowball in this self-directed hell."

Melea put her arm around him forcefully. "I refuse to allow you to dwell in negativity. Let's go have some supper, and then I'm taking you dancing."

"I can promise I'll be poor company," he warned.

"You've tolerated me when I was bad company. I can return the favor."

Rachel felt desperate to reach her father and Gary that night. She managed to get onto the Internet after numerous attempts and had ten minutes to leave messages for her father and Gary before the connection was severed again. Gary's message made her want to go home before it was too late, but she was cut off before she could ask either of them to come and get her.

Precious Rachel,

I've been going nuts trying to get through to you. Your dad threatened to hit me with a blast from a water hose, but he's just as frantic as I am. I never realized how terrible it was for you not knowing how I was. It's made me even more certain about leaving the service if the ISC job comes through. I'm going to meet with a realtor tomorrow. I'll let you know how it goes.

I love you,

Gary

She began walking the base corridors in an attempt to unwind. She made three laps while sorting through her feelings. It bothered her that she didn't feel the pain of separation from Gary to the degree he said he was feeling it. There had been a time when she had been mad with anxiety whenever he had been called away. He had gone weeks without sending her any word and told her it was because of the nature of his mission. He hadn't realized Rachel had known pilots could always send messages home. Where they were sent from was just blanked out. That lack of sensitivity had bothered Rachel for a long time. Ultimately she had accepted it as something she couldn't change. Those thoughts led her to even more unsettling lines of thought. She had always believed love would be more than what she was feeling. She had thought being in love would consume her thoughts and her dreams. Gary felt like a safe haven in a time of uncertainty, but he wasn't the first thing on her mind every morning or the last thing on her mind before she went to sleep every night. She suspected she would never be the first thing on Gary's mind.

There appeared to be a party in the mess hall, and she was drawn to go inside when she realized it involved swing dancing.

It was something she had enjoyed since college and something Gary didn't like. The music drew her like a magnet, but it wasn't a dance style that could be done without a partner.

Melea saw her first and pulled Bryne to the side of the room. "It would seem you have something else in common."

"Why are you so driven to make this match, Mum? The woman acts as if I'm a rapist. She recoils whenever I try to touch her."

"Just talk to her, Bryne," Melea suggested. "You've gotten off to a bad start. That doesn't mean you're destined to an unsatisfactory ending."

He sighed. "You won't give this up, will you?"

"Not without a battle," she said serenely. "Come along. I'll go with you for moral support." She propelled him through the crowd to where Rachel was standing.

"Obviously you like swing music, Dr. Madison," Melea said pleasantly.

"I always have," Rachel said as she felt her face flush. "Is the rest of the team here?"

"Just the two of us," Melea said. "This is my preferred form of exercise, but Bryne is much more of an expert."

"Not really," he protested. "I competed at a very amateur level, but that was a long while ago."

"You two should dance," Melea insisted. "It will give my arthritic knees a rest." She gave Bryne's back a firm push that forced him to step forward.

"If you would like to dance, it would be my pleasure," he said slowly.

Rachel had been thinking of a diplomatic way to make her escape, but Melea caught her eye. Her gaze was almost pleading, and Rachel thought maybe the opportunity would ease the enmity between her and the team leader.

"This is one of my favorites," she told Bryne. She extended her hand and tried to suppress every reaction to his touch when his hand closed over hers. It was impossible. She was glad he turned to lead the way to the dance floor.

Then he renewed her sense of guilt. "I'm sorry for losing my temper on the boat. I very much wanted to have a congenial relationship with everyone on the team. I hope that will still be possible."

"I'm sorry, too," she said. "I was able to put the note you gave me aside until I heard you had asked me to join the team for reasons other than my linguistic skills."

"I can't undo any of those impressions," he said slowly. "I can only tell you they aren't true." They were forced into the dance at that moment, and further talk was impossible until that number ended. The next number and the one after it compelled them to keep dancing before they took a break. They were both breathless as they moved to the side.

"You're quite skilled, Dr. Madison," he said.

"You can call me Rachel," she said. "I'm usually on a first name basis with my colleagues."

"I'd much prefer having you call me Bryne." He moved to the bar and ordered two bottled waters. "One doesn't expect to be so warm in this part of the world."

She smiled involuntarily, and Bryne felt a surge of renewed hope. He saw Melea take her leave but knew she wouldn't expect him to take his focus from Rachel. The conversation between them moved easily and superficially while they quenched their thirst. They returned to the dance floor and spent two hours there. They were one of the few couples remaining at the evening's end. The bar offered another drink before closing down. They both took a cup of tea and rested in the nearly empty mess hall.

"I didn't expect to have such a good time," she admitted.

"I didn't either. I was sent into the fray by Melea. She sees herself as striving to improve my afterhours." He stared into his tea, seeing Arielle's face. "I must admit something. I was very drawn to you from the morning I first saw you. You reminded me of someone I was involved with many years ago. Not in how you look. It's more an aura both of you have — had. I apologize for letting that carry me away. When you've had something so special, you want to believe it could happen again."

She had been ready to protest that his motives had been compromised, but the words died on her lips as she absorbed what he was saying and the emotional weight his words carried. "What happened to her?"

"She died," he said. "It's still difficult to speak of it. We met at university. I asked her out with a note like the one I gave you so you can feel certain it wasn't intended the way you thought it was." He drained his tea. "Enough of that. I should walk you back to your quarters. We'll be leaving early, and I expect the journey to be rather arduous."

They had spent four hours together. Later, Rachel realized Bryne McAllister had made her talk about herself and had listened with great interest.

"Did you really read my dissertation?" she asked him as they walked back to her quarters.

"Every word of it," he said. "What gave you the idea of a root pictographic language?"

"You might not like my answer," she said. "The Bible. Have you ever read about Babel?" When he nodded but didn't say more, she continued with her explanation. "I was in Chile on a dig. They had just located a Chincarro cave, and it had more petroglyphs than had ever been found. For a long time, they weren't thought to have a written language. Now we think most of the language they left on exposed surfaces was eroded by the winds. They found a wall with pictographs inside a cave, and I spent months working on it. Do you know about the Chincarro?"

"What I've read," he said. "They were a coastal Chilean Indian tribe that dates to seven thousand B.C.E. I beg your pardon. B.C. They're famous for their mummification practices. I recently did some in depth reading on their petroglyphs. I believe the scientist authoring the paper was named Madison. Have you heard of her?" Rachel smiled.

"We really didn't know much more about them until we found the wall of pictographs. They looked like primitive Egyptian pictographs to me. While I was trying to translate them, I started thinking about Babel. The Bible talks about all the people coming together and working together to build a tower up to heaven. God confounded their language so they couldn't talk to each other anymore. The linguistic similarities are proof of Babel to me because they suggest that everyone on earth did speak one language when language was new. None of the pictographs are actually interchangeable, but the way pictographs encompass certain ideas is common to all the languages."

"I like your idea, but I don't expect you'll like my next question." He smiled to let her know he was verbally playing with her. Rachel had always enjoyed verbal games and smiled back. "You obviously believe the story of Babel at face value. That being the case, why would the creator of a people keep them from advancing? It sounds as if their god wanted to keep them as ignorant minions."

"I don't think that's it at all," Rachel said. "I think sometimes people can gain knowledge faster than they can assimilate it. They can become too impressed with their own power and threaten themselves with destruction. That almost happened to the industrialized world with nuclear weapons during the Cold War."

He looked startled as they stopped at the door to her quarters. "That's a very different way of looking at it. Not a tower built to heaven, but a people who equated themselves to their god. I hadn't ever thought of that."

She smiled into his eyes. "Thank you for the lovely evening."

"It was lovely. I'll see you tomorrow. Good night."

Inside her quarters, she was sorry the evening was at an end. If she had allowed herself to compare the evening with those she had spent with Gary, there wouldn't have been any comparison. It took a long time to sleep because her thoughts seemed to be racing around her mind. Twenty minutes after she had gone to bed, a knock at her door awakened her. Georges Christobal was there, and his expression made Rachel uneasy.

"Good evening, Dr. Madison. I thought I could take up where McAllister left off. We should know each other better." He reached through the partially opened door to touch her, and Rachel recoiled from his hand. His expression frightened her.

"It's very late," she said. "I think we should talk at another time. Good night." She didn't wait for his response, but she could feel his anger as he stalked down the corridor. She lay awake for a long time wondering if it were another omen of bad personal fortune if she accompanied the team to the dig.

Melea had to awaken her the next morning. She didn't ask about the previous evening, and Rachel didn't offer any information because she didn't really know what to say. She expected they would be leaving early but was told they would be delayed again because of the weather over the dome. Around the military base were the bright blue skies of a clear winter day. Rachel was sitting at a table on the observation deck when she saw several of the Navy divers go running through the snow in wet suits followed by Bryne McAllister dressed in the same. They reached a pool some twenty feet from the observation window and dove into it without hesitation.

"What are they doing?" Rachel cried as Melea came to join her.

"Being crazy," Melea said casually. "The South Pole Club I believe they called it."

"Can the Nobel laureate spell hypothermia?" Rachel said.

"It's a hot spring," Melea explained. "This whole area is full of volcanic activity. You'd have to go to Iceland to find more."

"A hot spring? I've got to see this."

She dressed in her wet suit with her ski attire atop it. The thermometer at the outer hatch told her the outside temperature was ten below zero, but it felt colder until she reached the hot spring. McAllister and the divers were obviously comfortable in the steaming water."

Bryne looked up at Rachel and grinned. "What an expression. You may have missed your calling. I could see you as the headmistress of a school for unruly boys."

"Do you understand how quickly you can become hypothermic when you're wet?" Rachel asked. At the same time, she stepped back because the steam around the pool was actually hot.

"I'm quite flattered that you care," Bryne said as he swam toward her. "However, there really isn't any risk. You should try it. You won't find a hot tub like this one anywhere else on the planet. Just peel off the parka and give us all a treat."

She reacted on the spur of the moment as if she were nineteen again. She quickly pulled off her ski clothes and dove into the water wearing her wet suit to the whistles and cheers of all the men. The water was wonderfully warm and enveloped her with its soothing high salt content. She surfaced beside Bryne who was still grinning. Her eyes were drawn to his body, which was well defined by the wet suit. His chest was as muscled as a weight lifters. His abdomen was as flat as a much younger man's. She quickly looked the other way.

"Welcome to the South Pole's polar bear club, Dr. Madison. You're really quite fearless, aren't you?"

"I grew up on military bases," Rachel admitted. "Life was one dare after another." She lay back against the edge of the pool and relaxed in the warmth. "This is great."

"Not as great as last night, but it will do," he commented. "However, I would warn you to only do this in Antarctica or Iceland. In other places these baths can be hot enough to scald you."

"May I ask for another geology lesson?" she asked as she treaded water near him.

"I'd be honored," Bryne said.

"How do volcanoes form?" He smiled

"You've stumbled onto my favorite geological field of study. Some of them arise from subduction zones. That's when one of our plates is pushed beneath another and melts because of being pushed nearer to the heat of the core." He demonstrated the plate movement with his hands. "Some of them arise from hot spots in the mantle. The cause of those is hotly debated, if you'll pardon my pun."

"What's the cause the volcanic activity here?"

"This is plate activity as it is in Iceland. It's a very unstable area actually and it contains some of the largest volcanic caldera on earth. One of them is Deception Cove near where we docked. Have you always been fascinated with volcanoes?"

"Always. When I was a little girl, my father was stationed in Japan for a year. We went to a place called the Island of Fire. I saw the volcano there erupt, and I've been fascinated ever since. This is the first time I've really understood why it happens."

"It was always what fascinated me the most in studying geology. If I were still in that field, I'd have to discover how to divert lava fields. The Island of Fire is beautiful, but if you like volcanoes, you should see Iceland. There's something incomparable about seeing lava shooting out of a glacier. If we were in London, I could show you an incredible video the UK survey team made there when I was studying for my degree in geology."

"You're very relaxed in the face of the delays," Rachel remarked. "I expected you'd be pacing the floor with impatience because of the weather."

"It can't be helped. Mine is a hurry up and wait business. Translating is much more predictable so I'll have to provide the excitement in your life." He reached high up on the bank and pelted her with a handful of snow.

Rachel screamed as the ice hit her neck, but she was very quick to retaliate and hit Bryne with several ice missiles of her own before they called a mutual truce. By then Melea arrived to cajole all of them back into the station. Bryne climbed out first offering his hand to Rachel and then holding her parka. The temperature had begun dropping, and it was an uncomfortable transition for Rachel even when she reached the inner base. She was shivering and miserable in her quarters when a knock resounded an hour later. Melea answered it and brought her a thermos.

"Bryne said this might help you get warm."

"He's crazy," Rachel chattered. "I can't believe I let him get me into an Antarctic swimming hole."

"You had a good time, dear," Melea said. "Protest all you like, but we both know you had an much fun as a child breaking the ice to go wading at winter's end."

The thermos was full of hot chocolate, and Rachel nursed the drink for an hour before she was comfortable. Melea brought her a late lunch, and Rachel fell asleep with the tray still beside her. When Melea returned the tray, she stopped by Bryne's room to see how he was. She was surprised to find him wrapped more heavily than Rachel. His flushed face told Melea he had a fever.

"You're ill," she observed. "I believe Rachel may be right in saying you're crazy."

"I've had a virus for the last couple of weeks," he admitted. "It's going away. I just didn't realize the temperature shift would be quite so dramatic." He took the cup of hot tea Melea poured for him and sipped it gratefully. "Has she said anything, Mum?"

"She's having a good time," Melea said. "I hope you live through this little mating ritual, Bryne. You're not a kid anymore."

"Bless you, Dr. Adams," Bryne said acidly. "I wouldn't have re-membered without your prompting."

She ruffled his still damp hair. "I love you, Bryne, so you'll have to tolerate the motherly advice whether you want it or not."

CHAPTER 6

Rachel made it to her crawler the next morning after everyone else had boarded. It was an uncomfortable moment to find herself sitting with Georges Christobal. Instead of having time to worry about his intentions, she was privy to a heated argument between Christobal and the team leader.

"If the drill has broken through the ice crust, McAllister, then why must we send a probe? It would seem more logical to begin exploration now."

"We don't know what we'll find," Bryne said tersely. "If there are ruins, they aren't likely to be stable. We could find ourselves becoming a part of history instead of being students of history."

"Very quaint," Christobal said. "Or cowardly. There is always some risk on site. Just how many digs have you participated in, Nobel laureate? Or are you all on paper?"

"I'm the leader of this dig on and off paper," Bryne said. His flushed face betrayed the emotions his voice concealed. "I was chosen because I have more field experience than most field archeologists and because my technology found these ruins. I'll decide when and how we descend into them. We explored most of Egypt using probes to guide us. When we didn't use them, the outcome was sometimes disastrous."

"I know the sources of your funding," Christobal said in a threatening tone. "If you don't get on with this, I'll let them know you're dragging your feet and then we'll see who leads the way to the discovery." He glanced at Rachel and closed his mouth tightly. His eyes raked across her body invasively. He was a physically intimidating man, and he didn't have any charisma to soften that impression. He had coarse black hair and black eyes that appeared to have no pupils because they were so dark. As Rachel tried not to stare at the enraged scientist, she was involuntarily reminded of the drawings of Satan.

Christobal hesitated for thirty seconds and then smiled at her derisively. "Perhaps you should decide who the leader of this expedition is before you decide where you'll be sleeping. Perhaps then you will find me more pleasing."

Out of the corner of her eye, Rachel saw Bryne begin to protest just as Christobal reached out to grasp her arm. She moved with black belt instincts to elude his grip and twist his arm behind him.

"Don't let my age or gender fool you, Dr. Christobal. I can and will take care of anyone who threatens me. International law is in effect here, and I'll file charges if you come near me again." She had control of him during her verbal assault, but the tension of his arm in her grip communicated the predatory nature of the Austrian. When she released Christobal, Rachel moved to the back of the crawler and sat with her eyes watching both men for the rest of the journey.

It was an uncomfortably silent journey. Bryne took out a computer and worked on a program for the duration. Rachel had the impression he was shutting out everyone until she saw him glance at her twice. She thought the glance was speculative but his eyes seemed to speak of something more, something she couldn't interpret. Rachel thought of the radio her father had sent. It had become more than a mode of communication.

The dome was almost indiscernible from the white landscape until they were entering it. The storm gales had covered it with a thin layer of ice. The entrance would not admit the bulky crawlers easily, and an hour passed while their drivers negotiated the narrow opening one at a time. When they were inside, the temperature had fallen to ten below zero from the prolonged equilibration with the South Pole's inhospitable climate. Even the team's quarters were barely above freezing and remained that cold until almost midnight. The only warmth was in Melea's greeting. Rachel was glad to communicate what had happened during her trip to the dome. Melea accepted the story calmly.

"Christobal is a very aggressive man, and Gibar thinks he may be dabbling in things that fuel his aggression." Melea glanced at Rachel's face and then said, "Recreational drugs, Rachel."

She felt foolish when as she realized the explanation was plausible. "That would explain it. I hope these door locks are strong." She thought of the radio again and then realized it might not do her any good because of the weather. Still she did unpack it and was very surprised to find the pieces of a porcelain gun among the radio parts. There were two full clips with the weapon. She put it together deftly and used duct tape to conceal it under the sink. She felt much safer when she went to bed.

Their military escorts departed early the next morning leaving the dome to the nine person team of archeologists and the six man construction crew. The construction was complete externally, but there were obviously numerous tasks to finish inside and four of the men were doubling as drill workers. Technically Rachel's presence wasn't required at the drill site, but she suited up against the ever present cold and went to observe. She was curious how the interaction between Dr. McAllister and Dr. Christobal would go, but the two men seemed grudgingly cordial.

When she arrived, Bryne was rigging a computerized probe for the one-hundred foot descent into the ruins. It was carrying a very powerful lighting system on its back and a state of the art fiber optic system. Bryne was all business as he lowered the probe measuring every centimeter of its descent. At 39.76 meters, the probe touched solid ground.

"Success," Bryne said. He manipulated several switches on a console, and an image appeared on the computer screen with startling clarity. "Record everything, Mason."

To the seven archeologists, the image was unmistakably that of a ruin. It was also clear that it was the ruin of a technologically advanced civilization. The probe had touched ground beside a pile of equipment. The pile closely resembled a console.

"Jackpot," Dr. Carson said.

"We've got to get down there," Christobal said.

"Let's map what we can first." Bryne glanced at Rachel. His expression and voice were businesslike. "Get your computer and plug into Mason's console. If we see anything written, I want you to start translating."

"I'll be right back." She left at a run, knowing her professional future was absolutely secure because of the magnitude of the find. When she returned, Mason's screen was filled with an image of an unknown language. She quickly inserted her cable and began copying the screens as they appeared in rapid succession.

"It's similar to Egyptian hieroglyphics, but these symbols are closer to Babylonian. She sharpened the image on her screen as the meaning of one line came to her almost involuntarily. "Man becomes a god." Her finger touched the screen almost involuntarily. "Ba Bell." She was trembling as she looked at Bryne McAllister. "This is Babel, Bryne. We've found Babel."

"A Biblical myth," Christobal snorted derisively. "There's no mention of it outside of Hebrew texts. There's never been any mention..."

"If the glyphs call it Babel, Georges," Bryne interrupted, "you can't change that based on your own beliefs. The name doesn't prove this was the place mentioned in the Bible. It would take more than a shared name to prove that."

Bryne continued manipulating the probe moving slowly down the tablet until a twisted mass of steel could be seen. From there, he let the probe's fiber optics guide him through a maze of fallen brick and metal. When it reached an intact door, he manipulated the remote until the probe was in the foyer of a large building. Three mummified corpses blocked its way. They were unmistakably humanoid. As the probe turned, more glyphs were visible over the door. Rachel quickly copied the image.

"Now the questions are what happened to cause the downfall of this civilization, and how was this ruin preserved," Carson said.

"It must have been domed," Bryne said. "We must be sitting on the city's dome. I'll keep mapping. Georges, get everyone together with climbing gear and masks. We'll go down just after lunch."

There was no need to urge anyone to hurry. They were all very ready to descend into the ruins. Rachel didn't expect to be included, but when she remained at her terminal Bryne looked back at her.

"You may go with us if you wish, Rachel."

"Don't tempt me," she said. "I'd really like to go."

"Suit up," Bryne said. "Mason's recording everything. You're the one who'll be telling us what messages they left. You should see the glyphs up close."

She left Mason attending the computer terminals and returned to her quarters. The suit Bryne had mentioned was a wet suit designed for Arctic divers. Over it she wore a ski suit insulated to thirty below. She brought the transparent veil and her camera with her. Bryne was still working at the console when she returned. He was already dressed for the descent.

"There are rations on the mess table," he said. "We'll go down in another fifteen minutes." He smiled as he recognized the waterproof camera. "I had the same thought." He indicated a very expensive digital camera.

"This doesn't seem real, Bryne. I feel like I need pictures to show myself I'm not dreaming."

"If you were, you'd be sharing my dream. I've been dreaming of this sort of find for about twenty years." He came to his feet and began pulling on his parka. "The probe says it's thirty below down there. We'll be glad for all this in thirty minutes but right now I'm uncomfortably warm. Go eat."

She wasn't hungry, which was just as well because she was hot enough to be mildly nauseated. That feeling passed quickly when Bryne and Georges uncapped the shaft and attached rappelling gear to the steel and concrete support nearest them. They gave each team member a headset and then Bryne entered the shaft. He kept a running dialogue with the team as he descended.

"It's a tight fit," he said. "Close enough to brace your back against one side of the pipe and walk down the other. The rope tells me I'm halfway down. Watch the seam at twenty meters. It's a bit rough. I felt hung up for a moment." There was a long silence when Rachel held her breath.

"We're in Babel," he said triumphantly. "Come along, Georges. Mason, can you see this?" Rachel moved to a position behind the computer expert and stared at the images Bryne's personal video transmitter was sending. A crushed world spread out around him. When he looked up, they could all see the dented and battered dome above him. At one time it had obviously been many stories high, but some unknown disaster had flattened it to a mere ten feet in places. "I wonder what it's made of," he said as if asking their question.

Christobal was already halfway down before the others could tear themselves away from the screen. Mason kept the computer focused on Bryne's transmitter, and Rachel waited with him until Melea was standing on the edge. It was the first time Rachel had seen her new friend look apprehensive.

"Melea, are you all right?"

"I can't go," Melea said simply. "I just can't. Go ahead."

"You can do it," Rachel encouraged her. "Just close your eyes while you're descending."

"I can't. It's too much like the other dig." She put a reassuring hand on Rachel's arm. "My skill will be analyzing artifacts. Go ahead. I'll be watching you as soon as I take off the ski suit. I'm so hot I feel ill."

"I did too, but this breeze cooled me off." Rachel attached the rope to her harness and straddled the shaft as she pulled the transparent veil into place. She said a prayer and stepped into the shaft. She had rappelled many times but not through a pipe. She felt claustrophobic for a few moments and hurried her descent to escape the confinement. She stumbled as she touched down, and Bryne caught her.

"I was expecting Melea," he said, smiling. "I could tell from the feel that you weren't that professor of archeology." The emotions evoked by his grasp were confusing. Bryne felt her stiffen and released her.

"There are quite a few glyphs carved into the doorways. I've sent them to Mason, but I thought you might want to photograph them as well."

"Thank you for catching me," Rachel said slowly. "I didn't expect the pipe to end so suddenly."

"It must have been your first descent by this route," he said. He moved easily over the rubble until they were in front of a building. The architecture was similar to an Egyptian temple, but the glyphs were again different. Rachel dropped to one knee to steady her hands and photographed them. At McAllister's direction, she moved from building to building making innumerable photographs. It seemed almost like a poorly lit movie set until she entered a building and stumbled over a long dead body. It was little more than a skeleton, but closer examination told her frozen shriveled flesh was clinging to the bones. Carson knelt beside her.

"It wasn't always this cold in these ruins," he said. "If it had been, they would have been frozen before they deteriorated. These buildings suggest a warm climate originally. I've taken soil samples. Tonight I'll start the analysis and see where on earth we can find the closest match. Of course, you're the linguist, but I've found the glyphs for Babel on almost every structure. Did you bring your Bible? We might need the reference."

"I don't leave home without it," Rachel said. Even as she spoke, she felt a shudder of fear. She didn't need to translate her feelings. Something told her she was in the Babel of Genesis, a world that had been disrupted by God.

CHAPTER 7

The ruins were obviously huge. Bryne took sonographic readings before the cold forced them back to their quarters for the night. He estimated the area they would be exploring initially was over a square kilometer. The ruins extended well beyond that area, but they were ice covered outside of the ruined dome. Bryne spent his supper hour working on a rough map of the area they had seen.

Rachel spent her supper hour rereading the chapter of Genesis that discussed Babel. By the time the drill shaft was locked down for the night, Rachel had read the eleventh chapter of Genesis twenty times. It read differently to her for the first time in her life. In verse six where God had said, "Behold the people are one, and they have all one language; and this they begin to do; and now nothing will be restrained from them, which they have imagined to do," Rachel could see a people who had developed advanced technology and ceased to honor the God who had created them. She hurried to tell Bryne McAllister, but she held back when she reached the dining room. Bryne was already reviewing the hard data of the other team members, and none of them appeared to be voicing their theories.

"Did anyone see any books?" Rachel asked when she joined the gathering at the table. "Even if they were a computerized society, someone should have owned an heirloom book. If I could get more examples of their writing, I could translate the language more quickly."

"I think we're in the heart of the city," Dr. Carson said. "I haven't seen anything that looks like living quarters. We've only

71

been down there six hours. We'll need days to identify how they lived."

"I'd like to bring up a body," Gibar said. "Even with so little flesh, some DNA should be intact. I'd like to run a comparison to the DNA database. We could scan the more intact bodies as we find them and define what anatomical differences they have."

"We need to find out if the freezers are up and running first," Bryne said. "If they aren't, the body might decay faster than you can analyze it. Put a thermometer inside one tonight and see how it holds." He looked at Dr. Carson. "You're starting the soil analysis tonight?"

"As soon as I leave the table." Carson stood. "I left my equipment warming up. The temperature fluctuations here affect more than pathology."

"I'll have the construction crew seal off the lab space so there won't be so much variation," Bryne promised. "Dr. Tolliver is already working there. He took samples of the brick and metal for analysis. Tomorrow he wants to get some of the dome. We'll be working together."

"I have taken samples to analyze the microbes, and I've also found roots in the dirt," Dr. Marquette said. "I should be able to give you a report on the DNA of both in forty-eight hours.

"I've pulled up a map of the tectonic plates surrounding this area, Bryne," Marquette continued. "I've also set up a seismic monitor. You know this area shows signs of instability."

"There's always plate movement in Antarctica, especially near the volcanoes. If you see any change from baseline, we'll need to keep a constant sonographic monitor going," Bryne said. "It would take us a minimum of ten hours to start an evacuation if the weather allowed us to try. I'd rather have two or three days notice."

"Is our dome built to handle quake stress?" Christobal asked. "Surely you considered that risk."

"It's built to handle up to a level six quake," Bryne said. "The specs are on the main frame computer. Check them yourself. We're three miles from a volcano, Dr. Christobal. I can't guarantee your safety, and I'm certain you knew the risks since you're an expert in your own right."

The smoldering resentment rose between the two men instantly, but both managed to contain their ire. Christobal stood.

"I have brought up what appears to be a hard drive from one of their consoles. Tonight I will try to adapt it to one of our computers. If I have success, I will summon you all in the morning."

Bryne ignored the Austrian scientist and turned to Melea. "I left a box of small articles I gathered from the floors of the buildings. I thought you could begin cataloging them and comparing them to artifacts from other cultures. I know Rachel will be burning the midnight oil when she sees what I found for her."

"Bryne," Melea said slowly. "I'm sorry about today. I thought I could do it..."

"We have enough people for the exploration, Melea." Rachel was surprised by how soothing Bryne's voice was. It bespoke an emotional commitment to the older woman. "Just work on the artifacts. I'll gather more in the morning." He spoke in Rachel's direction without looking at her. "I'll be anxious to get your reaction, Dr. Madison. Let me know what you think."

"I'll get started now," Rachel said. She was titillated into running to her quarters. In a box on her bed was a metal plate engraved on both sides with glyphs. It was almost a meter square in size. Rachel immediately turned on her computer and began pulling up the other glyphs. She split the page and began creating a glyph dictionary using the pictographs that were most easily deciphered. She had been working for three hours when a knock resounded on her door.

"Come in," she said and turned to see Bryne standing at the door.

"You do know how to set up an aura of suspense," he commented. "I've been expecting to hear from you for the last three hours."

"Why?" she asked.

"Because we have a very exciting joint project." He leaned against the wall. "You've made it very clear that you don't want my attentions, Rachel. I was just curious as to what you might have found. It must be obvious that your work is an integral part of this expedition." He smiled. "And as a Christian, surely you want to prove this is the Biblical Babel."

"You're very irritating," she said. As usual he made her smile with his expression.

"So I've been told and very often. Tell me. What do you think?"

Rachel indicated her computer screen. "I've been working on a pictographic dictionary. Where did you find this tablet?"

"A curious choice of words. You sound as if you're speaking of the Ten Commandments." He pulled a chair over beside her. "It was in the largest, most intricately carved building. I believe it was some sort of government facility. In the largest cubicle, I found this beside a structure that might have been a desk. At least one symbol looks the hieroglyph for god."

"Very good," Rachel said. "God of the heavens vowed." This is the glyph for people but it's a little different. It probably means all the people. This is like the Babylonian glyph to serve and then here's the glyph for the god of the heavens."

"So basically it says the god of heaven vowed all the people would serve him. What's this one?"

"It's like the glyph for Osiris so I think it's probably a symbol for a god of the underworld or maybe the earth itself since it's below heaven. Babel serves the earth and all the people. The god of heaven was angered and anger rose up against Babel. I can't read this yet, but this is the glyph for to live again."

"If we find Nimrod's mummy down there, I won't be bringing it up," Bryne joked. "I don't want to start the Antarctic equivalent of the curse of Tut's tomb." He scanned her face expecting recognition of his joke. "You've lost your sense of humor."

"You might not understand how I feel," she said slowly. "If these people were destroyed by God, I'm a little nervous in unearthing what they were. God didn't just arbitrarily kill off populations. He only destroyed people when they were incredibly bad."

"Oh, yes. I remember," he said matter-of-factly. "You need to remember that most ancient cultures found a supernatural reason for natural disaster. As you've admitted, there's no real proof of what you believe." He stood. "It's ten o'clock in Houston, and the radar looks like another storm is coming in. You might want to get on the world network while you can."

"How did you know about that?" she asked.

"I asked Melea what my chances would be if I pursued you around Antarctica. She was equally straight forward and told me it was something like a snowball's chance in hell." He opened the door and then looked back. "If my chances improve, do let me know." He felt a micro burst of hope when Rachel came to the door. Those hopes were quickly dashed when she put her Bible in his hand.

"Read about Babel. It's in Genesis chapter eleven. The words are enough proof for a great many people."

"Thank you. As always, I'll keep an open mind." He left wishing he had stayed longer and not knowing Rachel was feeling the same regret. He made her feel as if she were a vital part of the expedition. She had never been made to feel essential to anything. She closed the glyph folder she had created before logging onto the internet. She expected to contact Gary, but he made no response to her instant message and the e-mail he had sent her was from the previous day.

Rachel,

I'm missing you terribly. I wish I had asked you to come home. I waited an hour hoping to hear from you tonight, but the radar showed the storm was still over you. I didn't realize we wouldn't be able to communicate for days at a time. When you get home, nothing is coming between us again. I love you.

Gary

She was disappointed because he had missed their date, but the e-mail helped. Ultimately she poured out her heart to Gary by e-mail telling him about the find and her trip in the crawler. It took a full sixty seconds for the tome of her feelings to be transmitted. Then she was emotionally exhausted and went to bed. The sound of the wind pummeling the dome awakened her twice, and she vaguely heard Melea return to their quarters. She dreamed her mother came in the room and put a gentle hand on her shoulder. She could feel her mother's breath on her face and hear her whispering a prayer.

She had dreamed about her mother often so she didn't look for any hidden meaning in the dream. She never knew Melea was the loving mother she thought was in her dreams.

In Houston, Colonel Madison was making one of the most distasteful calls of his life. It was to see his future son-in-law after hours because what he needed to ask Gary was definitely outside of their professional lives. He had his answer before entering Gary's apartment. When Gary answered his knock, he was dressed only in his uniform pants. A young woman was just behind him with a sheet clutched around her.

Gary's mouth dropped open on seeing Colonel Madison, and he stepped out into the hallway. "This isn't how it looks," he said lamely.

"I just needed to know," Colonel Madison said simply. "I had heard rumors, and I was stupidly denying them. I hope you'll be man enough to tell Rachel how you really feel. We both know this doesn't jive with saying you love her."

"Are you going to tell her?" Gary demanded.

"If you don't, I'll have to. I do love her," the Colonel said sharply. "We both thought you were a different kind of man." He walked away ignoring Gary's sputtered protests and praying for Rachel. He feared the knowledge would break her heart when she was alone among strangers. Ultimately, he chose to keep the truth to himself and prayed for God to help his daughter make the right decisions about her future.

CHAPTER 8

The team members were closed off from the world for almost three weeks while an Antarctic winter storm beat down on the dome. No one in the dome really cared about the weather because they were able to work in the ruins. It only mattered at night when they were unable to contact the outside world. By the end of their first week in the dome, they knew the continent had once been a part of the African land mass. Contrary to common belief, the land mass appeared to be more similar to the eastern side of the African continent. Bryne began a series of drawings of the tectonic plate movements necessary for the land mass' position.

Bryne had taken samples of the dome and used his skills as a geologist to analyze its composition. It was constructed of a transparent aluminum and silicon alloy.

"The patent on this alone should be worth several million dollars," he told Melea. Most of the metals were alloys as Bryne characterized them, he was gleeful. All of the compositions were different than those identified at other sites. They found transport vehicles and pieces of an ultralight metal that had been used in flight.

Rachel was drawn to watch the team leader work. He was without question the most brilliant scientist she had ever known. After watching him analyze their findings, she came to know that he wasn't gloating when his hypotheses were proven correct. He was expressing the giddy, boundless joy of discovery. It was the same rush Rachel felt every time she was successful in translating new hieroglyphics. After three and a half weeks of being around

Bryne McAllister, she began to look forward to any opportunity to be with him. She told herself it was to learn from him even when her heart told her it was something much deeper than a professional relationship being woven between them. She was the one seeking Bryne McAllister out because he had kept his word in not seeking her out after hours. When she found herself thinking of him whenever they were apart, Rachel was forced to realize that she missed Bryne's company more than she had ever missed Gary's.

She was running the evening Bryne was analyzing the metal they had taken from the aircraft. She paused at the laboratory door to watch him. After a minute, she realized he was alone. She wondered if she should disturb him or if he would want her to enter the lab when he was so intent on his work.

"You can come in," Bryne said without looking at her.

"I don't want to bother you," she said.

"I'm getting close to the wait and see stage," he said. "And I'm not on a tight schedule."

Rachel smiled. "I love the way you say that word."

He smiled broadly. "That being the case, I'll strive to say it more often. I see you like to run."

"It's better when the scenery isn't so bland," Rachel admitted as she toweled her face. "What did Armand find on the plant life?"

Bryne gestured toward the botany station. "This was a jungle at one time. Equatorial life without the markers of a slow transition. It fits the idea of polar shift. He's doing the DNA now."

"Melea did some isotope dating today," Rachel said. "She says the artifacts are more than ten thousand years old. She's guessing they're closer to twelve thousand."

Bryne moved around her to a machine she had never seen and peered through its binocular scope. "Your father will love this discovery," he said. "Have a look."

"What am I looking at?" she asked as she peered down at a crystalline structure.

"As best I can tell, it's an alloy composed of magnesium, aluminum, and silicon. It's ultralight, heat resistant, and strong enough to build a rocket. We don't have anything quite like it in the 21st century." He smiled at her. "A.D., that is."

Rachel smiled and sat down on a counter. "What else are you doing?"

"Just characterizing all the metals and rocks. I'm wearing my geology hat tonight." He shut down the crystallography station and collected his photographs and print outs. "How long have you been running?"

"Tonight or is this a life question?" she asked.

"Your choice," he said as he moved to the chemistry station and pulled the print outs from that computer.

"I've been running about twenty minutes tonight. I've always liked to run for exercise. I'll probably make three more laps around the complex unless you've found another hot spring where I can swim laps."

"Not just yet, but if you want me to look, I will. We're at the foot of an active volcano so there are probably some hot springs around here. Forgive me if I don't join you. I shivered like a dog for the remainder of that night."

"I'm glad I wasn't the only one. The hot chocolate really helped. Thank you. You're very considerate."

"Don't tell anyone," he said lightly. "You'll ruin a reputation I've cultivated for years." He put his data in a folder and turned off the lights. "Would you allow me to accompany you on the last three laps? I could use the exercise, too." When she nodded her agreement, he dropped off his data at his quarters. While she was waiting for him, she noticed a disc player and a number of music discs on his nightstand.

He ran the remaining three laps with her, proving he was in very good shape physically despite being twelve years her senior. He kept up a steady conversation during the run which was also proof he ran frequently enough to have built up his lung capacity.

"Why do you want a terrible reputation?" she asked.

"I couldn't really bear company after my friend died, but I suppose I've always been a bit of a loner. I was orphaned at a young age and grew up in government custody. It tends to make you distrustful. The bad reputation keeps people away if they just want to know the Nobel Prize. You'd be surprised at the effect that has on some people. I don't want to suggest that some women are gold diggers, but people can have a clear agenda I'm not privy to. I didn't expect to pursue another relationship and have my own reputation stand in my way."

"I don't think that gossip bothered me until you gave me the note. Most of the people who warned me about you said you were ruthless in achieving your career goals."

"I prefer to think I'm competitively driven," he said with a pained expression. "Ours is a cut throat business, Rachel. I've garnered millions of dollars in grants for this project. I have supporters because I've been successful in my past efforts. If I allowed myself to fail, they would fade much more quickly than the civilization below us. However, there are things more important to me than success."

She could almost see his thoughts moving to Melea. "You didn't really invite Melea for what she could do," she blurted out. "You have a special relationship between you. You knew this wouldn't be easy for her because of her husband. Maybe you knew it would help her heal." She caught a glimpse of Bryne's face and saw a fleeting image of personal grief.

"She has been a very close friend for many years. I was a student of her husband's, and I was with them on the dig when her husband died. I also enjoy her company." He slowed his pace as they approached the kitchen. "May I treat you to a cup of tea?"

She followed him as her answer and sat watching him while he brewed it.

"Do you work all the time?" she asked.

"I suppose I do. It never seemed so because I derive great satisfaction from what I do." He put a cup in front of her. "My life has been devoted to my work. I'm really quite boring otherwise. You may deny it, but you're very devoted to your own work. I've seen your face when you're translating."

"I love translating," she admitted. "I hope we can find some books in Babel."

"There's not much organic material down there," Bryne said. "It was probably flooded at some point so paper and leather would have decayed. I'll keep looking. There's always a chance. I saw a statue base today with a lot of hieroglyphics. I'll try to recover it for you tomorrow."

They walked a lap to cool down before stopping at the living quarters. On the way, their conversation strayed to personal issues again.

"Why did you say you're boring otherwise?" Rachel asked.

"I'm one of those crusty, old bachelors. I don't even have pets or plants in my house because I travel so much. I would have to schedule time for a social life."

"I'm sure the university has a social life for the faculty," Rachel said.

"Not one that I care to share. It's quite strange when you suddenly find yourself longing for something you didn't believe you would want. One day you're home and you realize how empty your house... and your life is. You think it isn't too late for intimacy, but it's not so easy to find someone who has interests in common with you when you're a scientist and past forty. Many of my colleagues get around that by marrying their secretaries or teaching assistants to have a trophy wife who's young, lovely, and familiar with their profession. It doesn't seem to matter that she can never really be a companion. If they grow apart, there's an amicable divorce and afterwards, another trophy wife. I wouldn't want that sort of relationship. I'd rather be alone."

"I don't think what you've envisioned is impossible." Rachel used her towel to wipe Bryne's face and suddenly couldn't meet his eyes because she knew she was settling for much less. Gary wasn't her friend. He rarely had time to listen to her hopes and dreams. His interests had always come first. Suddenly, she knew he had been saying only what he thought she wanted to hear. As she thought of the marriage proposal she had anticipated for months, she knew it had been tainted by Gary's jealousy or it wouldn't have come after she had left. She looked into Bryne's eyes and saw a longing she had felt too often while with Gary.

"I saw some music in your room, so I know you have some outside interests."

"I do like music," he admitted. "Do you?"

"Very much. What do you listen to?"

"If you don't mind sitting outside my quarters, I'll play some of them for you, I don't want to taint your reputation with my own. Or is it too late for you?"

"I'm not really sleepy," she said. She didn't want their time together to end.

They went to the corridor outside his quarters, and he brought out a disc player. The music was a surprise. It was a New Age recording from the 1980's by a group called the October Project. He played her a song called <u>Return to Me</u>. It was hauntingly beautiful. One verse in particular caught her. It said, "I know what it means to be lonely and I know what it means to be free. Now I want to know how to love you. Return to me."

"It's wonderful," she said. "I wouldn't have thought you would like something like that."

"You don't know me," he said. "You only know what my CV says and what other people, who don't know me, have told you. I would like for you to know me better, but I didn't think that was an option."

"Anything is possible," she said uncertainly. "Play another disc."

They sat in the corridor playing his music as if time were unimportant. Half his discs were selections she owned. It was unexpected to find they had so many things in common. In discovering who he was, Rachel felt as if she were finding who she was meant to be. The only downside was an aching need to be closer to him. When another song was conducive to dancing, she stood and extended her hand to him.

"Dance with me." Her commitment to Gary hovered between them like a specter. It couldn't keep her from shivering when Bryne's arms closed around her. It didn't keep her from wanting to hold Bryne closer than the dance necessitated. Their bodies fit together almost too well. Because it was a slow dance, there was nothing to keep her attention aside from how Bryne made her feel. When the music ended, they were looking into each other's eyes. She could feel Bryne was ready to kiss her, and her commitment to Gary came between them.

"I guess we should call it a night," she sighed.

"I hadn't thought of the time," he said. His face told her he could have continued their makeshift date even longer. "Thank you for an unexpectedly splendid evening."

"I enjoyed it very much," she said lightly.

"Sleep well, Rachel." His voice caressed her name. She could feel his eyes on her as she entered her quarters, but the feeling wasn't invasive. She turned back to smile at him before closing the door.

She had forgotten it was her birthday. When she went on the world network in an effort to contact Gary, the date on her computer reminded her the day was June eleventh. She was thirty years old. Her sister had left an elaborate birthday message. Her father had left a message wishing her a happy birthday. Gary had left almost the same message he had left daily about looking forward to her homecoming except the end of the message was a stilted statement saying he had argued with her father. He asked that she not talk to her father about their relationship. It was a message that left her wondering what was happening in her absence. It was obvious Gary had enough occupying him to make him forget her birthday. On impulse she printed the notes he had sent her every day and compared them. They were so similar that it became obvious he was rotating four notes. Only the greetings and the good byes kept them from being identical. She knew there were many emotions keeping them together, but love was not one of them.

She was feeling horribly depressed when she signed off the world network. Then she saw the envelope under her pillow. She thought it would be from Gary, some sort of elaborately planned surprise. Instead she found a piece of stationary inscribed with calligraphy. The card read simply, Happy Birthday, but attached to it by a ribbon was a small ancient coin. Beneath the coin, it was signed Bryne. Rachel closed her hand around it and finally slept with the tiny coin on the chain of her cross.

Bryne was as good as his word and brought Rachel the plaque from the statue the next day. When he had finished his work that night, he came to watch Rachel work on translating the new series of hieroglyphics. She had everything spread on the dining tables and was working intently, but she felt a surge of pleasure at seeing the team leader.

"Will I bother you if I work in here?" he asked tentatively.

"Not at all," she said shyly. He sat quietly watching her with his work in front of him as she constructed one sentence after another. She had a habit of whispering her results to herself like a child phonetically sounding out words.

"You're faster than any hieroglyphic translator I've ever seen," Bryne said with admiration. "Neill says you do it genetically, you know." Rachel smiled and stood to stretch her neck and back. When she sat down, Bryne moved behind her and began massaging her shoulders. His touch was unexpectedly stirring, and she tensed slightly.

"I'm sorry," he said quickly.

"No, it's all right," Rachel said. "I just wasn't expecting it. It feels nice." She relaxed against the pressure of his hands. "Neill hasn't ever known a Mayan who wasn't a tour guide on a dig," Rachel said. "I'm sure he told you my mother was Mayan. He tells everyone that."

"Does it bother you?" he asked. "If so, I won't mention it again."

"No," she conceded. "Actually I'm proud of it. My mother worked for the Bureau of Antiquities in Mexico. She was a tour guide at Uxmal. That was how she met my father. He was on a cruise with some of his Air Force buddies. She drew their tour. She never went farther than high school and tour guide training, but she had studied on her own. She used to take us to the ruins and show us where her people had lived. Did you ever see any of the Mayan ruins?"

"I flew to Guatemala and Honduras to see Copan and Tikal last month. I've never seen Uxmal." His hands were making her relax and wish that he wouldn't stop touching her.

"It's so incredible," she said. "You can stand at the governor's house and see temples rising out of the forest. I had this feeling of belonging to those ruins. I'm dyslexic, and my sister is, too. When I was being tutored on reading, my mother took me to Tulum and showed me how the Mayans had written and read from right to left in pictures. 'Don't worry about the dyslexia,' she said. 'You're just reading the way our people always have read.' When I started to work with hieroglyphics, I told people my skill was genetically acquired."

"I should be able to counter with some equally interesting story about my own background. Unfortunately, there isn't one. I'm simply the descendent of tree worshiping Celtic Druids. We were quite good with stone working. Have you seen my family church at Stonehenge?" He sat down facing her.

Rachel laughed as she closed her computer. "Are you ever serious?"

"Twenty-three hours a day," he replied. "We're near the bewitching hour when that facade begins to wear thin." He took her computer and walked her to her quarters. "Seriously, have you seen Stonehenge?"

"On the usual tour. I wanted to really examine the stones so much I could taste it."

"That was the site of my first dig. If you ever come over, I could show it to you inside the ropes. It's an amazing place. It has an aura about it that's hard to explain. An inexplicable sadness in the midst of awe. There are cremated human remains there, you know? We don't know if they were being buried there or were sacrificed. Of course it was built by an earlier people than the Celts, but the people of that time obviously engaged in human sacrifice if you look at the bodies we've found in the peat bogs. That bothers me even now. I'd much rather find the relics than the bodies. I think the whole idea of people being murdered to please the gods has made me feel more negatively about religion."

"The Bible taught against human sacrifice," Rachel said. She couldn't forget that Bryne's family had been sacrificed to her God and felt uncomfortable meeting his gaze. He didn't seem to notice.

"You never miss an opportunity, do you?" He stopped at her door. His next question made her feel as if he really wanted to know what her opinion was. His tone was curious rather than challenging. "Have you thought of how many people have died for the sake of Christianity? How many Mayans were killed so Spanish priests could convert the others? How many worlds were destroyed to save their souls?"

"Those things happened in the name of Christianity and not in the spirit of Christ. You have to think about what it's worth to live again, Bryne. Every civilization has looked for a way to live beyond this life. From what I've read, that's what Stonehenge was about. It was a way to let the spirits of the dead move into the moon. The Chincarro mummified their dead and carried them around to give them eternal life. Look at what the Egyptians did to see an afterlife. It's so much simpler than that. Knowing God will let you know eternity. I don't think God approves of the atrocities committed in His name, but that doesn't change the reward He's promised us if we obey Him. The nature of humans is to be violent even in their worship. My God tells people not to do it."

Bryne started to respond and held back because he didn't want his beliefs to come between them. "You're very eloquent. I'm certain you were a debating team champion. I'll concede the point for now."

"How did you lose your faith?" Rachel asked.

"How do you know I lost it?" Bryne countered. His face softened as her eyes pressed the question. "Very well. I saw suffering happen to people who were begging their God for deliverance. I can't conceive of a benevolent deity allowing his followers to die with their prayers unanswered."

"You don't know that their prayers weren't answered," she said gently. "God doesn't work on our time frame, Bryne. Sometimes prayers are answered in the next life." Her eyes held him, and he made no response to her challenge. She took that opportunity to push him further.

"Was it because the woman you spoke of died? Was she a Christian?"

He looked startled. "You're quite good with deduction. She was. I was raised in state custody so I had no religious ties. She did. She spent a great deal of time trying to persuade me to believe. I did listen. Then she died."

"Sit out here with me, and let me read to you, Bryne."

"Because I'm irresistibly attracted to you, I can't say no." He didn't meet her gaze when he accepted. They sat in the corridor between their two rooms while Rachel read the story of the creation to him. Bryne found himself unable to listen to her voice without feeling an emotional response.

"Can't you imagine it?" she asked. "I can close my eyes and see the universe coming from God's hands."

"I never have, but I'll have to admit you're a very talented reader," he said. He had a painful sense of déjà-vu. Arielle had given him a glimpse of heaven several nights before her death. He had told her he could believe that night. He knew it hadn't really been the truth. He had told her what she wanted to hear to get the answer he needed to hear. His voice was unsteady when he responded to Rachel. "It always seemed unreasonable to believe in something coming from nothing, but realistically that's what the revised big bang theory is. There was a moment when I was on the shuttle looking at the stars, and it seemed unreasonable to think something so perfect could have just appeared."

"Look at people, Bryne," Rachel said eagerly. "Look at how intricately we're made. It seems so unreasonable to believe we developed to this level by evolutionary chance. Think about the miracle of reproduction." She flushed and expected him to make some sort of comment, but he was silent.

"If I were going to believe, Rachel, it would be human emotions that would persuade me. I don't think the intricacies of DNA can explain how deeply people can feel for each other. I believe your Bible says God made us in His image. I would like to believe we only took the positive emotions from Him." He stood abruptly. "We won't settle this tonight. I'm keeping you up, and we'll have a long day tomorrow. Sleep well."

Rachel stood in the corridor watching him walk away and wishing they could talk all night. She hadn't ever wanted to talk to anyone else through the night. When he was well down the hall, she remembered the birthday card and ran to catch him. He turned on hearing her approach looking curiously hopeful.

"I forgot to ask," she said hesitantly. "Did you leave something in my room?"

"It was for your birthday," he said. "I remembered you were born in the summer and of course, I have everyone's vital statistics. It's not pleasant to be alone and not be remembered, especially on your birthday. I asked Melea to put it under your pillow."

"It was very nice of you," she said sincerely. "Where's the coin from?"

"From a dig in Jerusalem," he said. "A friend gave it to me a long time ago. It was the lowest valued coin in the first century A.D. It was what they called the widow's mite. I didn't have a great selection of gifts, and like the widow it seemed to be the best I had. I thought you would like to have it."

She stood on tiptoe and kissed his cheek. "Thank you. It means a lot to me. Really more than I can say."

His smile rewarded her. It was a very genuine expression and conveyed to her that he had put considerable thought into her gift.

"You're welcome. I was hoping you'd be pleased." When he was walking away, she realized how much more considerate he was than any man she had known other than her father. The only real barrier between them was his lack of faith, and she felt that would not always be between them.

She sat up translating until well after midnight because she wanted her work to impress Bryne McAllister. Then what she found fascinated her so much that she continued working. It became apparent that Babel had covered the earth with their travels by air. As Rachel looked at the photographs they had taken of murals in the ruins, an awful thought came to her. The people of Babel had favored ornate headgear. It reminded her of the many carvings of gods she had seen in South America and Mexico. By morning she was certain the similarity was more than a coincidence. She found Bryne before he descended into the ruins.

"You've got to see this," she said. "I've been working on it all night."

As always he was receptive and gestured toward the dining area. Rachel spread out the photographs paired with pictures taken at Mayan, Incan and Aztec excavations. The resemblance was too close to ignore.

"Do you know what this means?" she asked.

"Well," Bryne said. "It would seem the people of Babel dabbled in cultural contamination and set themselves up as gods. That would explain a great deal. So many primitive cultures were clearly monotheistic, and then we have these parallel cultures with advanced knowledge in mathematics, architecture and astronomy. They were all polytheistic and worshipped gods who brought them the knowledge from the sky."

"It's more than that," Rachel said. "You could go several steps further and say the people of Babel were responsible for all the sacrifices and bloodletting that came with worshiping them. All of these cultures believed the gods from the sky were coming back. Now it's easy to see why God put a stop to it." He ignored her last statement and continued to pore over the pictures.

"Good work, Rachel," he said finally. "You have enough here for a paper that will blow the lid off the next International Archeology Symposium. You're about to debunk all the UFO seekers. I'll drag up anything written I can find so you'll have more documentation. I've seen all sorts of gemstones and ornaments down there. I'll try to pick up some examples that would fit the contaminated cultures. That would be evidence they had been to the Americas and Egypt. You should start writing this up. I'd be honored to coauthor it with you."

His offer was a generous one. With a Nobel Prize winner's name beside her own, she would be assured of international recognition. She felt like a child rewarded by her parent for extra good behavior and spent the day translating feverishly. Everything she read confirmed her belief that Babel had blanketed the world with their knowledge and set themselves up as deities.

Bryne returned from the ruins that night with an incredible map cut in bronze. Tiny stars marked the sites of civilizations they all knew well. The Antarctic land mass was positioned between Africa and the Americas. While they were all pouring over the map, Bryne and Christobal had another argument over whether they should report their findings or not. The other scientists discreetly left the team leader and his problem child to argue it out. Rachel and Melea were gathering their materials to leave but froze as Christobal's attack turned physical.

"Listen to me, you Welch demigod. The scope of this find is greater than any other. We don't want anyone else coming here. We don't want publicity. We need to harvest every shred of technology available before the military sees what we have and comes in to take the site from us." His eyes narrowed. "Of course, you are a friend of the American military. Perhaps they have a vested interest in this project. Or perhaps you think that pleasing the military would get you the chance to screw Rachel."

"Say whatever paranoid tripe about me that pleases you," Bryne said without raising his voice. The intensity of his response was as frightening as Christobal's posture. "The final decision is mine. You're employed here. If you've forgotten that, let me remind you that you can be terminated. If you insult Dr. Madison again, I'll put you out of the dome to cool off."

Christobal sprang forward like an uncoiling spring and struck Bryne in the face. The attack put Bryne's back against the wall. Bryne was a smaller man but very agile. He obviously had martial arts training as well and struck Christobal three times in rapid succession to free himself. Then the two men stood facing each other, both ready to continue the battle until Melea shouted, "Stop this. Both of you."

"You'll live to regret this, McAllister," Christobal said. He shoved Melea out of the way as he left the room.

"He's gone too far this time," Bryne said. He looked at Rachel. "I'm sorry for what he said. I haven't said anything to give him that impression." His face softened at her expression, and he tried to lighten the moment by making it a joke. "At least not since you made your position clear."

Rachel's heart was still pounding in response to the terror she had felt for Bryne. There was a trickle of blood at the corner of his mouth, and she reached out spontaneously to wipe it. Bryne stepped back quickly and wiped it himself.

"I've had worse," he said. "Don't worry about it."

"I won't," Rachel said, feeling insulted and hurt by the gesture. At the same time she had to recall how often she had stepped away from Bryne McAllister. Suddenly the memory of his expression on the ship made her understand he was drawn to her on a kinship level and not just because she resembled his lost love. She was terribly confused by own feelings and turned away from him. "I'll just get some coffee and get back to work."

Bryne followed her into the kitchen and washed his hands. He used a damp cloth to press against his mouth. Then he stood watching her. Melea was behind them and left quietly.

Rachel turned back as the coffee brewed. "You don't have to wait for me."

"I was thinking of a cup of coffee myself," Bryne said. "I'm sorry if I hurt your feelings. You just shouldn't touch another person's blood bare handed. You can contract illnesses that way."

"Are you saying you have an illness?" Rachel asked.

He chose not to answer her question. Instead he leaned against the counter and was silent for several minutes. "I am sorry for what Christobal said. I'm sure professional jealousy engendered some of his lewd remarks, but it was wholly unprofessional for him to drag you into our disagreement. I don't think you realize how I've grown to respect you as a scientist. You've made a tremendous contribution to this dig already."

"I'm glad you asked me to come," she admitted. "You've really been good to work with. I've felt like maybe this dig is why I was meant to go into archeology." She poured two cups of coffee and put desiccated creamer into hers. When she extended a cup to Bryne, he closed his hand over hers in something akin to an embrace. She froze as Bryne's touch generated an incredibly powerful magnetic attraction. Gary's hand had never evoked such a feeling in her. The simple touch seemed to communicate the deeper undercurrent of feelings they shared. His eyes burned their way into her soul as his other hand closed around her hand.

"We've come back around to the first moment I saw you," he said. "I was drawn to you. I thought it was because you reminded me of Arielle. Every day it has seemed clearer that it isn't that you resemble her. How you make me feel is the similarity. I've never felt so strongly about anything before. I think your Bible calls that deep calling unto deep. It wasn't that I didn't want you to touch me. I very much want you to touch me. Not sexually. Just to touch who I am. Really you have been from the moment we met. Not just anyone can do that. I think that only happens if you've met your soul mate. I can't tell you how much I want that to be true."

The silence when he stopped talking was almost palpable. Rachel knew Bryne had opened his heart to her, but she couldn't think of what to say even though her heart knew. Her only rational thought was that she couldn't tell Bryne that she was in love with him until she ended her relationship with Gary. She had to look away because she couldn't continue meeting his gaze without expressing her feelings.

Bryne released her hand and stepped away. His expression told Rachel she had hurt him more than she had ever hurt another person. She felt as if she had shoved a dagger through his heart. She reached out to him but not before he turned away. He never saw her response to his pain or her hand reaching for him. Rachel knew he was walking away in an effort to conceal his raw emotions.

"Don't work too late." She could feel his pain in his voice.

She watched him walk from the room realizing he had been touching her heart a little more every day. She had to force herself to return to her quarters and not to follow him to apologize. She couldn't risk letting him see that he had already succeeded in making her love him until she had settled her relationship with Gary and until she had assured herself that Bryne could share her faith. She walked into her quarters like a sleep walker and sank down on her bed. Melea was working on a piece of sculpture and glanced at Rachel furtively as she entered their quarters.

"You've swept Bryne off his feet, Rachel," Melea said quietly. "I don't think he's used to feeling that way. Actually I'm sure he isn't."

"You know I'm engaged, Melea," Rachel protested. "I can't let things go too far when I've committed myself to Gary."

"You've already let it go too far," Melea said. "Bryne is fragile, Rachel. He has lost everyone he ever loved, and he's been afraid to let himself get that close again. He let it happen with you. He didn't want to, but he told me he was helpless to close you out. Are you definite about Gary?"

"I'm supposed to get married when I get home," Rachel said slowly. "I haven't been able to talk to Gary since we arrived at the station. Even our communications over the worldwide web have been letters back and forth. I can't let anything develop between me and Bryne until I settle what's between me and Gary."

"Then tell him that. He will be agonizing that he did something wrong, and I don't think he'll ever try again." She saw Rachel did not understand and said, "He was engaged to marry my daughter, Arielle. She was vivacious and never met a stranger. She pursued Bryne. They looked enough alike to be brother and sister, but they were very different at first. It was like watching a flower open to the sun for the first time. Then Arielle and my husband were lost on the dig. Bryne took care of me as if he were my son. I will always love him for that, but I know he never let go of his anguish. He doesn't have the comfort of faith to help him let go."

The words told Rachel that Bryne had been reaching out to her from their first encounter. Even the hieroglyphic note took on a new and charming meaning. It was the gesture of a man who was reserved and afraid of showing his feelings. When she heard his words from that evening in her mind suggesting they were soulmates, she wanted to cry.

"I'm so confused," Rachel said. "I thought I knew what I wanted, and now I feel lost. I don't know how to make him understand."

"Just telling him how you feel is a good start," Melea said. "I think I'll go walk for a while. Sleep well." As soon as she was out of the door, Rachel went to the computer and began trying to access the World Wide Web.

Melea walked to Bryne's quarters and knocked until he answered reluctantly.

"The proper response is to invite me in, Bryne," she suggested.

"Even if I'd rather not, I suppose." He stepped aside and gestured toward the room. Arielle's picture was lying on the bed near Rachel's Bible. Melea moved to lift her daughter's picture and smiled at the laughing face.

"This was my favorite picture of her. Rachel has the same sort of joie de vivre." Melea looked at Bryne speculatively. "Do you see that in her?"

"Sometimes," Bryne said, "I think I should have avoided Rachel like the plague for that reason if for no other. People are so worried about the consequences of brief physical affairs. I can tell you they aren't nearly as stressful as having your emotions turned inside out on a daily basis."

"That's the risk of loving someone, Bryne," Melea said. "No matter how much it hurts, it's certainly better than a lifetime of emptiness and physical affairs."

"I'll concede to the lifetime of emptiness, but I want you to know that the physical affairs have been nearly nonexistent," he said. "I've been with three women in my lifetime. Two of those were before I was twenty. I don't like that sort of behavior. It gets you nothing more than the moment." His face was ineffably sad. "I never slept with Arielle. I would have waited for her forever."

"Arielle wouldn't have wanted you to be alone, Bryne," she said. "She would have wanted you to be happy. We both know you aren't. Would you erase what you had with Arielle even if you had known she was going to die?"

"No," he said simply. "Sometimes my memories of Arielle are what keep me going." He took the photograph and put it on the nightstand. "Just now that's definitely the case. I've let myself fall helplessly in love with Rachel. Tonight, I told her how I feel, and I'm certain she doesn't share my feelings. It was like losing Arielle all over again. I feel very alone, Mum. More alone than I've ever felt. I wish I knew I had some chance of making that feeling end." He pressed his hand against his eyes. "I never could understand how my mother felt after my father's death until Arielle died and then again tonight."

"You don't really know how Rachel feels, Bryne. I'm certain she feels more than you think. She met you when she was already in a relationship, and she isn't the kind of girl who betrays another person's trust. Put it in God's hands and believe He will hear your prayers."

"I'll try to believe in what you're saying, Mum, but I don't know if I can ever believe in a benevolent deity who took Arielle away from us. How can you?"

"I only survived it because I believe in God and an afterlife. I know they aren't really gone. More than anything else, I want you to believe it as well."

He put his hand over hers. "Why have you bothered with me for all these years, Melea?"

"Because I love you," she said simply. "I see you as my son, Bryne. I see everything Arielle loved about you. I know she wants me to look after you." She bent to kiss his cheek. "You aren't always easy, but nothing worthwhile is ever easy. Come with me. I'll make you some tea."

"I can't." He squeezed her hand. "I'm all right, Mum. I'll be all right. Get some sleep." He walked her halfway to her quarters and returned to his room. When he lay down on the bed, he held Rachel's Bible on his chest. When the quiet became overpowering, he opened the worn leather book to the page marked by a red ribbon. The words Rachel had underlined were, "Ask and it shall be given." He felt a rush of unreasonable anger that God could be forcing him to beg for help. He closed the book forcefully and put it aside.

Rachel had been unable to reach Gary. She had left him a message asking for contact the following evening, but it seemed a lifetime away. It seemed so clear that she had never loved Gary. He was an attractive, charismatic man and very successful. He had always been confident about their relationship. He had known she was committed to him and had taken it for granted. He had called her precious, but he had never made her feel precious to him. When she thought of the word, precious, she could almost see Bryne's eyes telling her, "Maybe that only happens when you've met your soul mate."

What kept her from sleep was an aching need to go down to his room and apologize for not saying what he had needed to hear. Then she wanted to tell him that she loved him. Before she could sleep, she prayed a long time for God to show her what to do.

In Houston, Colonel Madison left the base very late that night. He had been delayed by attending Gary's funeral. He had gone only because of Rachel. Gary had been involved in a car accident several days earlier. He and the woman with him had died from their injuries. Arthur Madison went home and began trying to reach his daughter. He planned to tell her a very limited version of the truth.

CHAPTER 9

The jangling of the alarm clock jarred Rachel awake. She had forgotten what time she had set on the clock and sat up in the dimly lit room to see the glowing red numerals. Before she could absorb the time, she realized the room was very cold. Melea was wrapped in two blankets and shivering.

"Someone must have breached the dome in some way," she chattered. "The temperature has been dropping since two in the morning."

"We need to find out why," Rachel said through clenched teeth. She took all the bedclothes with her to reach the closet and the ski bib and parka she had worn the previous day. "The water will freeze soon, Melea." She brought the older woman her outerwear. "Let's go see what happened." While Melea was dressing, Rachel tucked the gun into her clothes.

The corridors were empty until they reached the area near the drill site. All the men were in that area working feverishly to seal off the opening to the ruins from their living area. Mason was the only man not physically working. He was at his console concentrating intently on the computer's screen. Rachel leaned over his shoulder.

"What happened?"

"Christobal went down into the ruins sometime last night. He couldn't close up behind himself, and the drain of trying to warm the dome and the ruins overloaded the generators. We have emergency power for the next four hours only. The external temperature is one hundred below zero. It's thirty-two in here now. McAllister says it will drop twenty degrees an hour with the emergency power source."

"What are you doing?" Rachel asked, trying to suppress the fear in her voice.

"I'm looking for Christobal. He took his transmitter, and he should be in range. I can't pick up a signal."

"How cold is it below?" Melea asked.

"Around forty below," Mason said. "If he's still alive, he won't last long."

"What can we do?" Rachel asked.

"Ask McAllister," was Mason's terse response.

Rachel hurried to find Bryne. He was making an effort to seal the drill site with the hatch. Because it had contracted in the cold more than the drill shaft, it wouldn't fit tightly. Bryne pulled it out and wrapped it with another layer of thin metal.

"What about rubber?" Rachel suggested. "There were some deflated tires just inside the dome when we got here."

"They're equipment tires we blew while we were building the dome," a worker explained.

"Get one," Bryne said tersely. He peeled off the metal hurriedly and then followed the worker. Both men returned with a tire. The worker brought a machete like knife, and they split the rubber long ways. They wrapped it tightly around the hatch fastening it with rivets. When they pushed it into the shaft, it fit tightly making a seal.

Both men were on their feet moments later and ran toward the generator room. Rachel followed them praying they would be able to remedy the power loss.

"Check an internal temperature on generator B," Bryne told the workman. "I think A is burned out."

"What's the power source?" Rachel asked hesitantly.

"It's a fission/fusion generator," Bryne explained. "It should have been a self regenerating fuel supply, but when it overheated, the reaction changed. We still have hydrogen in B but I don't know how much yet."

"The internal temperature on B is seventy-five," the workman said. "The specs say that's safe for start up."

Bryne moved over the controls like a concert musician. "Get me a fifteen micron particle stream, Braden."

"You've got it," the workman said.

"Fifteen seconds to ignition." Bryne's eyes were on the gage monitoring the particle stream. "Eleven, ten, nine, eight, seven, six, five, four, three, two, one. Ignition."

Both men hit a series of buttons, and after an agonizing fifteen seconds, the generator settled into a steady whine. Bryne leaned against the console and exhaled slowly. The workman patted his shoulder. "If you want that physics degree, sir, I'll tell them you did your dissertation under fire."

"We've still got to get the other one running before I've earned it." He looked at Rachel. "Would you and Melea mind getting some food thawed and making some coffee? We've got about ten hours of labor ahead of us conservatively, and neither of you can help us with this. Braden, get on the radio and asked the military people to bring a containment core if they have one to spare."

Braden returned as Bryne was tearing down the second generator. Rachel came into the generator room bringing a cup of coffee as Braden delivered the message from the military base.

"There's another storm coming in, Dr. McAllister. We won't be getting any help from the base until it breaks. I could barely hear them over the interference."

Rachel saw Bryne's face and knelt beside him to give him the cup. "We're in trouble, aren't we?"

"If I can't get this going, we're in trouble," Bryne conceded. He sat up and drained half the cup gratefully. "You don't know anything about generators, do you? The tire idea was a life saver."

"I don't know anything about generators." She hesitated and then sat back. "We need a containment core?"

"The core in A was destroyed. I've been working on B since the alarm sounded at two this morning. If Christobal is alive, I may kill him myself." He drained the rest of the cup. "We can't really jerry rig a containment core because the 'fallout,' pardon my pun, of a failure would be very unpleasant. One generator can keep us alive, but we won't be doing anything but sitting in a room together."

"A core could be dropped to us, couldn't it?" she asked.

"You mean from air support?" Bryne asked. "Yes, if we could radio someone with enough authority to get it done." He scanned her face. "Why?"

"Come with me," she said. "Don't ask. Just come."

She led him to her quarters where the temperature was already intolerable. Bryne stood at the door as Rachel entered. She opened the duffel bag and took out the radio. Bryne swore under his breath.

"Your father's with ISC," he said as if explaining the radio to himself. "That wouldn't lock onto satellites, would it?"

"It would." Rachel flipped the switch and adjusted the frequency. "Colonel Madison, come in please." She repeated the message three times and then her father's voice came across very clearly.

"Rachel, I've been trying to reach you. How's the expedition going?"

"Dad, we've got a big problem. One of the other team members went into the ruins last night and left the dome open to the native environment. The power drain melted down the core of one generator. We've got to get it up and running or we'll be in big trouble. We can't get help from the base because of a storm. Can you have a containment core air dropped over these coordinates?"

"Yes," Colonel Madison said. "Do you have the specs, Rachel? I'll need everything you can give me."

"I'm going to put Dr. McAllister on, Dad," she said. Bryne took the microphone gratefully.

"We very much appreciate your help, Colonel Madison," Bryne said. "It's a Corex series 6978 for the two million watt capability generator. If you could drop two, it would be safer because the other one also took a beating last night."

"We'll have to drop them by parachute," the colonel said. "I'll put them as close as possible to your dome. We'll use red parachutes for better visibility. Give us twelve hours."

"Beggars can't be choosers," Bryne said. "I'm very grateful." He returned the microphone to Rachel.

"Thanks, Dad. You're a godsend."

"I wish I had talked you out of going," the colonel said. "Rachel, I was trying to get you for a reason. I wish I didn't have to tell you, but you'll know soon enough."

"What is it?" Rachel said with a whisper of fear.

"Gary is dead, Rachel," the colonel replied. "He was in a car accident six days ago. The other driver lost control of his car and crashed into the driver's side of Gary's car. He only lived a few hours. The funeral was yesterday. I'm sorry, sweetheart."

Rachel sat down hard clutching the microphone but unable to speak into it. Her feelings couldn't be encompassed by a single word. The most overwhelming was her guilt because she had prayed for a way out of the relationship.

"Are you all right, Rachel?" the colonel asked.

"I'm all right," she said numbly. "I'll be all right. It just doesn't seem real. Tell his parents I'll be praying for them."

"I will, Rachel. I promise." The radio went silent, and Rachel flipped off the switch mechanically. She thought Bryne had left the room until his hand closed over her arm gently.

"I'm sorry. I know that isn't much help, but I am sorry. I won't tell you that I know how you feel. That sort of tripe made me angry when I lost Arielle. If you need a shoulder, mine is available." He pulled her to her feet. "You'd better keep that radio hidden. We may need it again."

They walked in silence to the generator area and parted company. Bryne returned to dismantle the broken generator donning a radiation suit before he exposed the core. A Geiger counter told him that the fuel had been completely exhausted. Only minimal gamma radiation showed on the meter. He wondered if his emotions were responsible for the few clicks on the machine. He had felt a surge of hope on knowing Rachel's fiancé was dead. The hope had been dashed by his own second thoughts. He felt guilty for being glad another man had died. He was still crushed by the thought he could do no better than being Rachel's second choice. He wasn't sure he could live with that feeling even if Gary's death drove her into his arms.

Rachel and Melea manned the kitchen tasks, and everyone else completed the construction of sealing off the drill shaft area. At dusk the area was carefully secured so that no one could go in or out of it without Bryne's help. The temperature in the dome's center was forty degrees. Their compartments and the labs were sealed off against the greatest cold near the dome's outer wall. The team made their beds in and around the generator room to wait until morning and the lifesaving containment core. Only Mason kept working. At midnight Rachel moved to watch him because she didn't want to sleep. Every time she closed her eyes, all she could see was Gary's face. She kept remembering her prayer to decide between him and Bryne McAllister. She felt as if she had betrayed the man she had promised to marry. At the same time, she was aching to be with Bryne.

"It's almost Sunday morning," she told Mason. "I wish we could have church."

"I'm a minister," Gary said quietly. "I used to have my own church. After my wife and I lost our first baby to congenital heart disease, I just couldn't preach anymore. We'd been praying for a baby for three years, and then we had Adam. He lived eleven months. I left the ministry. All day I've been thinking I made the wrong decision." He sat back and stretched. "Let the others know we'll have church in the morning."

"Say a prayer for me tonight," Rachel said softly. "I'm having my faith tested."

"Have Bible, will travel," Mason said. He took a pocket Bible out of his parka and turned to face Rachel. "I think this is a 23rd Psalm moment."

They recited the Psalm together and then held hands to pray. They didn't know Bryne had come to the doorway, awakened by their voices. He sat down outside of the generator room and listened to words he could still remember. "Though I walk through the valley of the shadow of death, I will fear no evil for You are with me." For thirty-four years Bryne had hated the sound of scripture being read, but Rachel's voice made him want to hear it. He found unexpected comfort in the words.

When they sang the hymn, <u>Be with Me Lord,</u> Melea came to join them and then Dr. Carson moved his bed closer to listen. Their church service lasted for two hours, which didn't seem long enough. When they had finished their worship Rachel felt calmer.

Through her tears, she stared at Mason's screen and saw a blob of red on the blue field.

"What's that, Mason? It wasn't there before."

"It's a heat source," Mason said incredulously. "Two hundred feet down." He moved the screen around and the red blob persisted in every position. Mason recorded the position and looked at Rachel. "Wake Bryne. He needs to see this."

Rachel found Bryne sleeping just outside the door, but he awakened the moment she touched his arm. She was surprised to see her Bible was beside him. He returned it to her as he stood and followed her into the generator room. He was likewise bewildered by Mason's screen.

"What sort of heat are we talking about, Mason?"

"The colors represent differential temperature," Mason replied. "I'd think this might be body temperature. Maybe it's Christobal."

"If it is, his survival skills rival anyone's on this planet," Bryne said. "We can't go after him tonight. It's too risky to pull more cold air into the station. He made his bed. He'll have to lie in it. I wish I knew why he went."

"What about the hard drive he was working with?" Rachel asked. "He said he found a hard drive in the ruins."

"I don't know," Bryne said. "Maybe we need to know. I'm going to search his quarters. Come with me, Rachel. I may need translation help."

She followed him feeling glad to have any distraction. The intense cold almost made her change her mind. When they were inside Christobal's quarters, Bryne gave her the blankets from the bed before taking a seat in front of Christobal's computer terminal. A large piece of alien appearing equipment was wired to a port. When Bryne called up the screen, a video began playing slowly. A man dressed in flowing robes and elaborate headgear appeared as if photographed seconds and not millennia before that moment. He spoke to them in foreign words.

"Play it back," Rachel said as she focused on the words.

"This program is designed to conform to the user's language," the figure said in English. "We are the people of Babel. This is a message to those who find what we were. This message will let us live again. Not even God can destroy us. We are as gods ourselves. We drew all the people to our land east of the Tigris and Euphrates rivers. We learned all the secrets of the universe. There was nothing we could not do. We have flown around the earth and reached out to the stars. God said to us, 'Worship me and only me.' We said we have no need to worship when nothing is beyond our ability. We were generous. We visited people all over the earth and gave them knowledge. They worshipped our gifts to them. The god of heaven only gave them words. We gave them power. The god of heaven is a jealous god. He sent a plague on our people so that we could no longer speak to each other and understand. Our scientists developed this program to allow us to communicate. We learned to speak to each other again and worked together to have the power of gods. Then God said to us that we must repent or be destroyed. Great earthquakes came. Volcanoes brought forth fire. We built a domed city to survive. We found the way to live again if we do not survive. If you are seeing this program, you are the vessels to resurrect Babel. Welcome to the world of the divine. Welcome to the world of gods." A map flashed across the screen. "Follow us to eternal life." Bryne pressed print and then replayed the message speaking to the screen in German. The screen displayed numerals one through twenty and said the words for each in a foreign language. Bryne said the words for the numerals in German. Then the screen showed several objects and named them. Bryne named the objects in German. The screen progressed to showing a person walking, eating, carrying a block. When Bryne spoke the German words for the actions, the being reappeared and repeated the message in German.

"I wouldn't have believed it if I weren't seeing it," Bryne said. "This is obviously something Christobal found and not something he created." He put the map on the screen again. This is a map of the ruins. Can you read these glyphs?"

Rachel moved closer and scanned the symbols. "Some of them. This means the fire of Osiris. This is the glyph for to live again. If I work with this program and give it different ancient tongues I might be able to learn their language."

"Let's take the whole set up then," Bryne said. He carried the computer while Rachel supported the hard drive. He set up a station for her in a corner near the generator. It was the warmest area in the room. He brought his own computer and sat near her. Often she knew he was watching her work rather than doing his own. The only thing that distracted her was a growing feeling of oppressive fear. When she took a break to rest her eyes, she asked, "Did you read Genesis chapter eleven?"

"Several times," Bryne said. He knew where she was headed and tried to divert her. "There are some intriguing coincidences with our ruins."

"I know you don't want to believe there could be a supernatural explanation for their demise, but the dating doesn't coincide with any known asteroid strikes. Why couldn't God have caused tectonic plate shift?"

"If there is a God, I suppose He could have," Bryne said slowly. "I'm not so arrogant that I feel I have to know how the plate instability occurred. We don't have time to delve into the metaphysics now, but I am thinking of it, Rachel. My answer should be an assurance that I'm not a liar. I want to say what you want to hear, but I can't do that."

She didn't know how to respond to him. His face told her he was grieving. She knew it was because of her and couldn't think of what to say. They were the only ones awake in the station, and the only sounds were the hum of the generator and the wind against the dome. They both heard another sound overhead, and Rachel smiled.

"A C30 just flew over us," she said.

"Your father to the rescue." Bryne closed his computer. "It's 4 A.M. He's right on schedule. He has the reputation of being a man who gets things done."

"He does get things done at ISC, but he's so much more than his title. He was an astronaut and a pilot. He was in a bad accident, and he grounded himself to make sure he'd be around to raise me and my sister. Our mother died eleven months later. She had an aneurysm and it ruptured. Daddy was our mother and father until we went off to school."

"That's not a usual father or the usual man." He looked at her, and his expression was unfathomable. "Are you going to be all right, Rachel? About your friend's death?" He wouldn't meet her gaze, and she knew he was pushing her away again.

"I'm just trying not to think about him." The rush of tears came before she could stop them, and she put the computer aside and left the room. In the cold dining area, she shook with the sobs she had held back for more than twelve hours. Strangely she couldn't fathom why she needed to cry. Her feelings were a swirling maelstrom of guilt and grief for losing what she had felt with Bryne. He was suddenly beside her, putting a blanket around her shoulders. Then he put his arms around her. It was a comforting embrace. Rachel turned in his arms and rested her face on his shoulder. He stroked her hair as her father might have. His hands were gentle, and she wanted to remain safely in his arms.

"I'm sorry," he said. "I shouldn't have asked. I was just worried about you. Death affects people in unpredictable ways. People you see as very strong can see their lives as being over. I wouldn't want anything to happen to you."

In the midst of her own pain, Rachel realized he was talking from his past and what had happened to his mother. "I'll be all right," she whispered. "I don't question what happens to me. I know I'll get through it. I just wish I could talk to him one more time. There were things we needed to say." She stepped back and wiped her eyes with the blanket.

"There are always things left unsaid. I still think of things I wish I had said to Arielle. Melea told me she survived the loss because she believes in an afterlife. I've wondered if there is such an existence, can the people there know what has become of their loved ones? I would like to tell her how sorry I am for not being with her that day.

"Melea's husband, Arthur, was my mentor after I finished my postdoctoral work in archeology. I signed on with their dig under the Sphinx to have more field experience and to be with Arielle.

"We were in Egypt searching the chambers under the Sphinx. The dig was physically very challenging because ground water has flooded all the chambers. The government has been trying to pump them dry for years. Arielle and I were doing most of the diving. I cut my arm during a dive, and it became infected. I developed a high fever, and I was really quite sick. It was a Pseudomonas infection. People die from that sort of infection even in this day and age. I was treated on the site with intravenous antibiotics because I refused to leave. I wish I had allowed them to take me to the hospital in Cairo. If I had, Arielle would have been with me. I wanted to go with her that day, but I was still running a fever and had an open wound. She talked me out of going. I never saw her again." He stopped abruptly and was silent several moments.

"She was everything I ever wanted and all the things I know I'll never have. If the truth were told, I would give back the Nobel prize this instant to relive those days in Egypt to a different end." He looked at Rachel with open pain in his eyes. "To answer the burning question in your heart, we weren't ever sexually intimate. It wasn't necessary. To me being in love means caring so much for another person that your own life doesn't matter anymore."

She didn't know how to respond to the story. "I don't think I could have kept Gary alive," Rachel said for Bryne's sake and her own. "I think people have a time to be born and a time to die. We had a terrible argument before I left home. After I got here, I realized the argument was a sign of the problems between us. I tried to reach him last night, but I couldn't." She realized she felt jealous of how Bryne still felt about Arielle. She also knew she wanted and needed him to have that same degree of feeling for her because she had dreamed of being loved completely. His response was carefully formulated to push her away.

"That's from Ecclesiastes." He offered her a cup of tea and was careful not to touch her when he gave it to her. "Don't look so surprised. I have read the Bible. It's a very important piece of history and literature. I can't prove your God doesn't exist, but if He does exist, He has allowed a great many innocent people to suffer. I find that difficult to understand. I'm very certain I don't believe in miracles or answered prayers because when I have prayed, my prayers were ignored. Now I probably don't merit being heard, but I was also ignored when I was a child begging for help."

"Have you ever thought the fact that you survived means God heard you. I believe faith can let you see the reason things turn out as they do. That's the book of Rachel." They both smiled almost involuntarily, but Bryne's smile faded quickly.

"I broke my word to you. I've pursued you since you arrived. I let myself believe there was a mutual attraction, but now I know— I appreciate your honesty, and I won't bother you in that way again."

She couldn't think of how to respond. She realized Bryne was closing the door on their relationship and knew what had happened the previous night had made the decision for him. Even though she couldn't blame him, she couldn't bear losing him. She felt very desperate as she moved closer to him.

"You don't understand how I feel, Bryne," she said. "I've been drawn to you from the first time we met even though almost everyone has told me I shouldn't be. I didn't know what to believe about you. I think I had to learn to believe in you and not your reputation. We have so many things in common..."

"Please, don't," he interrupted. "I don't want to feel that way again. I want to finish this dig and allow all of us to enjoy the success."

She moved toward him involuntarily reaching out. She put her hand on Bryne's face without any forethought and caressed his hair. His skin was warm under her hand. His eyes were mesmerizing as he looked at her.

"I thought you were taller," she said. It wasn't what she wanted to say, but she was afraid to open her heart when she hadn't allowed him to open his to her.

"It's the Nobel prize," he said. "It makes the rest of the package seem much grander than it actually is." He turned back to get his own coffee dislodging her hand deliberately. He stepped away from her and inclined his head toward the generator room. "You should get some sleep now and so should I. I'll have to be out as soon as I can tolerate the cold and find your father's air shipment. We're in the long night part of the year. I'll only have a few hours of daylight."

He was telling her not to touch him, and Rachel felt sick as she followed him to the generator room. The emotion was much more intense than anything she had ever felt with Gary. She felt as if she were losing everything she had ever wanted. She trailed Bryne hoping he would turn back to take her hand or put his arm around her, but he stayed away from her. She spoke to him out of desperation before they reached the point where the others might hear.

"Bryne, please don't walk away from me. I'm sorry about last night. I know I hurt you, and I didn't want to hurt you. There were things I wanted to say."

"Don't say them now, please," he said without looking at her. "I don't like feeling pitied. If we had a relationship now I would always remember I wasn't your first choice. I'll be fine, Rachel. I just wanted something that isn't meant to be. You shouldn't feel guilty for telling me the truth."

He went back into the generator room because he was losing control of his carefully controlled emotions. Rachel didn't understand she was tearing him to pieces with her plea. She felt rejected and then devastated. She couldn't bring herself to follow him. She wanted to cry, but she felt too empty to generate the tears. Then she sank down at a table and cried with much more emotion than she had felt or shown for Gary. She didn't know Bryne could see her. She didn't know she was communicating something he needed very much. Her heart rending tears told him that she was feeling as lost and confused as he was. She cried until no more tears would come and shook with sobs after her tears ceased. Bryne was ready to return to her when she left the dining area because she couldn't bear the physical chill any longer. She was still wiping her eyes when she moved quietly into the generator room. The other team members were asleep, wrapped in their warmest clothing and every cover they could find. Bryne was lying in the room's darkest corner. She couldn't see his face or know that her expression was giving him reason to hope. She glanced at the thermometer before she crawled into her sleeping bag. It read just above freezing, and she shivered uncontrollably from the cold and the emotions her tears had not been able to dispel. She was feeling unrivaled despair until Bryne moved to lie just behind her.

"Sometimes you have to do what you must to survive," he whispered. "Then you try not to enjoy the sacrifice." He put his arm across her, and the warmth of his body seems to envelope her with hope.

"Thank you," she whispered. She moved until her back was touching him and gradually felt comfortable lying close to him. It was very difficult not to turn into his embrace even though she had never slept in a man's arms.

"I'm enjoying your sacrifice," she whispered. "I can't help myself. I hope you'll eventually be able to forgive me. Sometimes it's hard to see the truth of how you feel, Bryne, even when it's right before your eyes." She almost held her breath as she closed her hand over his arm. She felt him tense and prayed he wouldn't pull away. When he didn't, she moved even closer to him without knowing the painful pleasure she was evoking. She held his hand between her hands as she relaxed and closed her eyes. In the quiet darkness, she prayed for God to bring them together because it felt so very right to think of spending her life with him. She was able to sleep without Gary's specter and the guilt of her divided feelings haunting her. When she turned over in her sleep and rested her face on Bryne's chest, she didn't hear him whisper, "Please," into the darkness.

CHAPTER 10

Melea shook Rachel awake early in the morning. She started shivering as soon as she turned back the covers.

"They've found the parachutes," Melea said. "The site is at least a mile away on the side of Erebus." Her face was anxious. "Bryne's getting ready to go."

"Who's going with him?" Rachel asked with equal anxiety.

"I think Gibar is," Melea said. "We need to get the medical facility up and running in case they have problems. Have you had EMT training?"

"Yes, but I've never needed it." She realized she was more afraid for Bryne McAllister than she had ever been for anyone else. She felt as if her own life revolved around his. Melea's face said they shared that concern. "How cold is it outside?"

"Seventy below," Melea said.

"They can't walk that far in this cold." Rachel came to her feet and hurried into the dining area. Bryne and Gibar were pulling on extra layers of clothing. They both looked apprehensive. Rachel went to Bryne.

"You can't possibly get there and back on foot, Bryne. Don't we have any sort of transport?"

"One snowmobile," Bryne said grimly. "We didn't think about needing to be outside the dome. The weight limit is three hundred pounds so it won't carry two men with or without the cores. I don't know that I can lift them alone."

"I weigh one twenty in all my gear," Rachel said. "I'd guess you weigh one sixty. We could rig a sled to pull the cores behind us. We'll be going downhill coming back." Bryne hesitated.

"I don't think you know how cold it will be on the mountainside, Rachel."

"I've climbed Mount McKinley," she said.

"OK." He smiled. "Maybe you do know." Bryne looked at Gibar. "Work with what we have and keep the shaft locked off."

"I will." Gibar was obviously relieved to be excused from duty. He peeled off his parka.

"What's the oxygen concentration on the slopes of Erebus?" Rachel asked.

"At that temperature it's probably about 17%. We have tanks and masks."

"Are they heated?" Rachel asked. "If we use heated oxygen, it will cut down on how much body heat we lose."

"We can heat them for about an hour. Suit up and I'll get them. Armand, get the snowmobile out of storage chamber three." Bryne paused to squeeze Rachel's arm. "Put on everything you have to insulate your hands and feet." He held up his left hand and revealed the absence of his left fifth fingertip. "That's a souvenir from climbing Everest. I was about your age. Experience is an unrelenting teacher. Book of Bryne."

Melea followed her to their quarters and held a radiant heater on Rachel's body while she dressed in the wet suit and then five layers of socks and an insulated shirt and pants. Over those she put her ski bib, parka, three pair of gloves and her boots.

"Be careful, Rachel," Melea said. "I don't ever want to lose a friend on an expedition again."

"Bryne told me about Arielle," Rachel said as she laced her boots. "I didn't know."

"He loved her. She loved him." Melea sighed. "I don't know if I would have lived through losing them both if not for Bryne. He was there when I most needed him." She paused. "Don't lead him on, Rachel. He deserves better than that." She turned off the heater and moved toward the door. "I'll set up the infirmary while you're gone."

Rachel pulled on her gloves and then impulsively embraced Melea. "I'm in love with him. I've never been more sure about anything. I just couldn't reach Gary, and then I didn't know what to say."

Bryne's appearance silenced Melea's response. He was almost unrecognizable in his heavy suit with a full face mask, headset and oxygen tank. He gave the same equipment to Rachel, and she donned it expertly. As she fastened her parka, Bryne spoke over the microphone.

"We need to go. There are storm clouds blowing in, and the temperature is starting to drop. We only have two hours of daylight. Are you ready?"

Rachel raised her thumb and lifted the other side of the snowmobile without being asked. They carried it into the airlock and waved to the other team members. She had time to pray before the outside hatch opened and a blast of wind almost took her off her feet. It was as if she didn't have on any protective gear. She hadn't ever felt such an intense cold.

"It's not too late to change your mind," Bryne said as he saw her flinch. "It will be even colder before we return." She knew she was probably being foolish to risk her life to accompany him, but she also knew his chances of survival would be greater if she went with him. That thought solidified her resolve to go with him.

"I'm not afraid," Rachel said. "We have to do this. I'll be praying us back." His focus changed as he moved toward the snowmobile. He stopped thinking of anything except returning her safely home. Rachel climbed on the snowmobile behind him. Almost before she was seated, he gunned the engine and started into the wind. His body took the brunt of the wind chill and protected Rachel. She felt warmer as they moved into the bright sunlight. She was startled by how fast they were able to move over the ice.

"Where's the sled?" she asked with sudden remembrance.

"We made it from an aluminum sheet. It's rolled up in the snowmobile's storage compartment." His body felt very tense under her arms. "Are you all right, Rachel?"

"I'm fine," she reassured him. "How fast are we going?"

"Twenty miles an hour. We'll slow down going up Erebus. I'm hoping it won't take more than twenty minutes to get to the drop point. We can't go as fast coming back because of the sled."

"Are you all right?" Rachel asked.

"What more could I want? It's a beautiful day. I'm in the company of the loveliest woman for hundreds of miles. Finally, I've convinced you to touch me. I'd say today has already been a great success."

It was too cold to laugh. Rachel embraced Bryne without any hesitation, and he squeezed her arm in response. They skated into the wind sometimes getting up to forty miles when the wind released them. They dropped to ten miles an hour as they started up the mountain side. They had been exposed to the cold for thirty minutes when they reached the brilliantly colored red parachute. Rachel stepped off the snowmobile first and immediately fell. The snow was a frozen into a sheet of ice. She hit too hard to be able to audibly warn Bryne, but he was quick to recognize the situation. He ground his heel through the crust until his right foot was secure and then ground his other heel through before reaching out to help Rachel up.

"Are you hurt?"

"I bruised my ego," she conceded as she used his hand to get up. "We could use ice cleats."

"Hindsight," Bryne commented. "Well, perhaps that was a bad choice of words. Let's go."

They moved carefully over the ice to reach the package. It was frighteningly big, and Rachel wondered if she could lift her part. She was relieved to find much of the bulk was packing. The package weighed about one hundred pounds, and Rachel carried her part without much difficulty.

When they reached the snowmobile, they left the package to unroll the sled. The wind fought them making the aluminum sheet into a solar sail until Rachel had to sit on the sled while Bryne dragged the package to the sled. He fell once during the process, but Rachel couldn't help him without risking the loss of the sled.

The aluminum was wrapped around the package and fastened with brads. Bryne chained it to the snowmobile and climbed aboard. The heat on their oxygen tanks failed as they started back to the dome with the clouds trailing them. The sun was already beginning to set, and Rachel could feel the temperature falling as the cold began to overpower her. The wind was like a knife in her back. She didn't want Bryne to know she was suffering, but he felt her shivering.

"I'll stop and let you drive," he offered.

"You'll go faster," she chattered. "I haven't ever driven one of these." Her mind felt fogged, and she struggled to clear it.

"It's hard to believe this was a warm place," she said.

"It would have been equatorial. We would have been sweating and wearing loincloths. Now the thought of you in that attire warms me considerably."

She was too cold to laugh and too cold to think. She wasn't sure she could stay awake. She rested her face against Bryne's back giving herself to the waves of somnolence. They promised to carry her someplace warm. Bryne shook her arm hard.

"Wake up, Rachel. Don't prove me stupid for bringing a woman." His words were sharp and cruelly insulting.

"I was the only one with the guts to come with you," she protested.

"Then have the courage to finish the job."

The dome was just within sight when the waves of sleepiness began to wash over Rachel again. She was too cold to talk, and Bryne was too cold to make her talk. Every time he felt her relax against him, he shook her. They were still two hundred yards from safety when the snowmobile sputtered and then slid to a stop. Fear roused Rachel up.

"The fuel lines are too cold to allow vaporization," Bryne said. "Get off and push. If we leave it, the lines will freeze solid and rupture tonight."

Rachel stumbled getting off the snowmobile, but she gripped the handlebar and began pushing. She couldn't feel her feet or hands. Instead of making her warmer, the effort of pushing made her breathe harder. The cold oxygen seemed able to freeze her from the inside out. Bryne bore the bulk of the snowmobile's weight for the last hundred yards. Fifty yards from the dome, Rachel collapsed on the icy ground. She was unconscious when

Bryne put her across the snowmobile and battled his way across the remaining distance. He stayed on his feet until they were in the airlock, and then he collapsed beside the sled.

Rachel was unaware for a long time, and as she regained consciousness, she remembered a collage of sounds and sensations. Most vivid was the memory of Bryne leaning over her. She could feel his hand caressing her hair, but she couldn't open her eyes.

"Don't leave me," he said quietly. "Please don't let me have killed you. If there is a God, You can't let Rachel die."

She was startled to think he was praying. She thought she could feel his lips touch her forehead. His breath was warm on her face. She could feel his hand holding hers for a very long time. Rachel remembered wanting to comfort Bryne, but the task was too great.

Melea was sitting beside her adjusting intravenous tubing when she awakened. Rachel was shivering despite feeling the weight of innumerable blankets on her.

"You'll be shivering for a while yet," Melea said. "You were very hypothermic. Your body temperature was under thirty-one Celsius."

"Where's Bryne?" Rachel managed.

"Firing up the second generator. He's shivering nearly as much as you are, but he was determined to get that generator running. It's one hundred twenty below on the Fahrenheit scale outside." She pulled one of Rachel's hands from the blankets and immersed it in a paraffin bath. "You've got a pretty good case of frostbite on your fingers and toes. You might have died."

"God still wants me here," Rachel said resolutely.

"So do I," Melea said. She repeated the process with Rachel's other hand and tucked the blankets around her. "Sleep for a while and then I'll bring you some soup."

Rachel grasped Melea's wrist. "I dreamed Bryne was here with me. I dreamed he was holding my hand."

"He was here every second until we knew you were going to be okay. He only left to get the generator running." Melea stroked Rachel's forehead. "Sleep now."

Rachel saw Melea put something in the intravenous line and a wave of delicious somnolence washed over her.

"I love him," she whispered. She couldn't remember if she had actually said the words or dreamed saying them.

She slept dreamlessly until she was finally warm again. It was very quiet in the room when she awakened again. She sat up slowly and scanned the room. She wanted to see Bryne, and she quickly found him. He was asleep on a pallet on the floor. His face and hands were red and looked blistered in patches. He hadn't shaved in several days, and his beard was a gold colored stubble on his ruddy face. He looked younger than forty-one and vulnerable. Rachel felt a surge of maternal protectiveness toward him. That feeling was in stark contrast to the memory of his harsh words on the snowmobile and how he had pushed her away the previous night.

The intravenous line had been removed from her arm. Rachel slid off the infirmary table. She moved with the blankets still around her to sit down beside Bryne. He startled at the sound of her movement and sat up.

"Are you all right?" he asked with open relief on his face.

"Just tired," she said. "I guess I gave out on you."

"You almost made it into the airlock," he said. "I've been feeling guilty because I let you go. I was afraid I'd let you kill yourself."

"I wasn't going to let you alone. Anyway, I made it. God took care of me. I read a book once that said God hates cowards. It would have been cowardice to let you go on foot." It seemed important to know if he had meant what he had said at the end of their ordeal. He didn't give her the opportunity to ask.

"I shouldn't have let you go," he said. "I wasn't sure I could make it alone, but I'm the team leader. It's my duty to die if necessary to keep the rest of you alive. You were the only one with enough courage to volunteer, but I shouldn't have let you go."

His hands reached out to her and slid into her hair. His hands were hot on her skin as if they were bearing the emotions on his face. He pulled her close until she was in his arms. His mouth brushed hers as if to ignite what had been smoldering between them. With that one touch she knew what it was to want and need someone in a way she had never wanted or needed anything. The emotions passing between their eyes surpassed words. Only seconds passed before he kissed her, but Rachel was shuddering with the need to feel him when he gave way to his desire. The intensity of the kiss was like what she anticipated it would be to make love. His beard was rough against her skin, but she still didn't feel he could be close enough to her. She clung to him even when the kiss ended and kissed his throat as she rested her head on his shoulder.

"I had to be with you, Bryne," she whispered against his neck. "I had to make sure you'd be all right. I knew I couldn't bear it if anything happened to you. My life didn't matter anymore." She put her hands on his face and initiated their second kiss. She pressed her body tightly against his until she could feel he was shaking as much as she was. It wasn't in response to the cold for either of them. They were on their knees clasped so close that they seemed to be breathing in synchrony. She hadn't known love and desire could be so entwined. Bryne's sudden reaction was completely unexpected.

"I can't do this," he said as he pushed her away. "I'm not what you want. This is only happening now because you've lost the man you love. When we came here I thought I could eventually make you care for me, and instead I'm completely at the mercy of how I feel about you."

"Why couldn't you be what I want?" Rachel asked with anguish. "You are what I want, Bryne."

"I saw your face when I told you how I felt," he said. "I knew I'd never be the right man for you. When I knew Gary was dead, I was glad because I thought I might have another chance. Then I hated myself for making another man's life so trivial." He stood and was walking away until he heard her catch her breath in a choking sob of agony. The sound and what it meant froze him.

"I want to leave here as soon as the base can send someone to get me," she said. "I hope you'll help me leave here. I can't stay on the dig with you. I know it isn't professional to just quit, but I don't care. I shouldn't have come. I knew I was feeling things I couldn't understand, and now that I understand, it's too late for me to escape from loving you. When you told me how you felt, I had to accept that I felt the same way. I knew I was in love with you, but I didn't know what to say because I had promised to marry

Gary. I spent hours trying to reach him to break off our engagement. If you really cared for me, you wouldn't need to hear words to know how much I care for you. You should be able to look in my eyes and see how I feel. What you just said makes you just the sort of man everyone said you were. Everything is all about you. I'll pray for you, but I can't ever see you again. I couldn't stand it." She walked out the door, but she starting running when she reached the corridor. The rooms were almost warm in tribute to Bryne's success with the generator, but Rachel hadn't ever felt so cold. She had reached the living quarters when he caught her in the web of his words.

"Please don't go, Rachel," he called out to her. "I'm– I'm praying that you won't go. I'm sorry for all the things I keep doing wrong. I don't know what to say except that I need you. I need you to be with me more than I've ever needed anything in my life. I need to believe you love me, Rachel, because I love you so very much." She stopped moving but couldn't stop shaking.

"I do love you," she said, "but I can't be with someone who doesn't believe in God, Bryne. If you can't believe, I should go now before we hurt each other even more."

"I would do anything to have you feel about me the way I feel about you," he whispered against her hair. She hadn't felt him close the distance between them, and she shuddered involuntarily. His hands closed on her arms with desperate pressure. "I could fall on my knees and worship any power that would let me be with you, Rachel."

She pulled his arms around her and relaxed against his body. When she felt as if she could breathe again, she turned to look in his eyes. His eyes told her that he loved her. The words poured from her as if the dammed up emotions of weeks had been released.

"I don't ever want to leave you," she said. "I felt guilty about Gary because the night he died I was thinking about how I could break up with him. I prayed to know what to do because I knew— I know I've never loved anyone like I love you. When you said we might be soul mates, I knew it was the truth, Bryne. I knew I hurt you because I couldn't answer and tell you that I was in love with you without betraying Gary. You were never my second choice.

He was." His expression startled her because it communicated incredulous joy. He pulled her close and held her as if he wouldn't ever let her go.

"I love you, Rachel. There's just not any question about how I feel in my heart. When I wasn't sure I could get you safely back, I wanted to pray for you. I was praying to stay on my feet and get you to safety. I can hold you and believe prayers can be answered. Please stay with me always." The words were like a wedding vow between them, and they stood in the open hallway kissing and touching with feverish need. Bryne finally pushed her away gently and held her away from his body. "We have to stop, Rachel. I want to commit myself to you and not just give way to how I'm feeling now." His face clouded suddenly. "Come with me. I need to give you something."

She followed him to his quarters and was startled when he returned from the bathroom with two bottles of medicine. "I have a virus, Rachel. It's a CMV virus." His face flushed. "I'm ashamed to tell you how I contracted it, but I swear to you I'm not promiscuous. I hadn't been with anyone in a very long time, and then I was alone and thinking I was always going to be alone. I drank more than I should have." He shook his head. "I can't make any excuses. I don't know if you can contract the virus from kissing, but I think you should take these. I'm sorry. I didn't think about exposing you this way. I've been sending blood to my doctor, and he said I was almost clear last week. I just wouldn't want you to take any chances." She took the bottles and spoke from her heart.

"It doesn't matter, Bryne. I wouldn't have cared if I had known. My life belongs to yours now so we'll just have to share anything that happens to either of us."

"I didn't know I could feel so much for anyone," he said. He seized her with the force of his emotions, and she couldn't have pushed him away. Again Bryne stopped. "We may have to keep meeting in the corridor. If there were a way to be married tonight, I'd ask you to marry me now."

"If that was a proposal, I'm ready to say yes."

"Then tomorrow, we're getting married," he said simply. "No matter what else happens."

He held her hand as they walked down the corridor and kissed her forehead as they reached the door.

"I'm going to my quarters and take a very cold shower," he said. "Take your pills. Expect me to awaken you early." As she watched him walk down the corridor, she believed she could see her future more clearly than at any time in her life. She was too excited and happy to sleep and turned to her work to pass the hours until she would see him again.

For the rest of the night she worked through the alien message using the symbols for Egyptian hieroglyphics and then ancient Hebrew. On the later, she began to understand the spoken words. Then she keyed in the Babel glyph for to live again and the message expanded to a lengthy scientific document.

Bryne had felt euphoric, but he forced himself to sleep because beneath his feeling of emotional triumph was the knowledge that they were a long way from safety. He returned to Egypt in his dreams as if making the journey to say a final goodbye to Arielle. He was in a tent in the desert with the night winds flapping the canvas but not easing his misery from fever and heat. Arielle came to sit beside his cot and pressed a cold compress to his forehead.

"They've had great success with the water today," she commented. "Dad just finished surveying the outermost chamber. The hieroglyphics are extraordinary, Bryne. They're like the ones at Luxor. You could easily convince yourself there was once a civilization here with the power of flight."

"You're becoming a science fiction writer," he said irritably. "Don't read so much into the carvings, love. These people were obsessed with the most primitive ways of preserving their culture. That hardly suggests they had any amount of technology."

"I'm going to get my Bible and read to you about Babel," Arielle said with assurance. "You feel very comfortable in believing the Sphinx is more ancient than the pyramids. You can't know what lies under these sands any more than I can. I do know that I can almost feel what they were thinking. All the ancient cultures were driven to live again. They have so many commonalities that you have to wonder if there was a mother race living on Plato's Atlantis."

"Focusing on an afterlife across some mystical sea simply proves they weren't capable of analytical thought," Bryne said. He immediately knew he had said the wrong thing. Arielle stood and stepped away from his outstretched hand.

"I'm focused on an afterlife, too, Bryne. I had believed you were going to focus on that as well."

"I'm trying," he explained lamely. "It isn't so easy. My mother was focused on that goal when she killed my sisters and herself. It isn't easy to see that afterlife as paradise."

A voice called to her in the distance, and Arielle looked over her shoulder. "That's Mom. It's time for lights out."

"Stay with me," he pleaded. "I'll sleep on the sand. You can have the cot."

He could see the doubts in her eyes, and they frightened him. He could see she was losing faith in him and their future. "Arielle, please don't leave." She avoided his grasp.

"You know, Bryne, it's hard for you to believe in God because of the tragedy of your life. It's hard for me to believe in us when it's obvious you've been lying to me for the duration of our relationship. You say what I want to hear. Now I'm going to say what you don't want to hear. Your mother didn't kill herself and your sisters because of her faith. She killed them because she was too cowardly to believe God would take care of her. Maybe you need to blame her instead of God and realize that God is the reason you lived. You can either be a coward like your mother and live in a web of lies or you can start looking at your own history in a more rational fashion." She left the tent like a gust of wind. He had been too angry to pursue her. He saw past the night to the shrill screams awakening him the next morning. It was well after sunrise. He knew the voice was Melea's. He couldn't hear Arielle, and his sweat seemed to freeze as he ran toward the site.

He sat up panting in the darkness. He had tried to forget that night he had seen Arielle last. He had tried to forget that she had been angry and betrayed when she went into the underwater chambers. He had to accept that his lies might have driven her to her death. He went to the sink and washed his face. The sick feeling remained because he had lied to Rachel just as he had lied to Arielle. He had promised to worship her God. He still had lingering doubts that her God existed, but as he stood at the sink he saw Rachel collapsing on the ice. He felt his being begging for help to save her and the unexpected surge of strength that had filled him. That surge had allowed them to survive. Scientific logic told him it was nothing more than adrenaline. Something deeper told him he couldn't have saved her without help. He closed his eyes and tried to feel the presence Melea and Rachel felt.

"I don't want to lose her," he said to someone or no one. "If you're there, show me how to keep her." A distant rumbling opened his eyes. He knew every expected sound and sensation in the station. The rumbling was a warning of something not a part of it. He took his own concealed weapon from under the sink and left his quarters.

A knock on their door awakened Melea. She brushed Rachel's arm, rousing her from staring at the glyphs on her computer screen as she answered the summons. "Who is it?"

"It's Mason. Bryne wants everyone to come to the drill shaft. Two of the construction workers are missing."

They showered hurriedly in water that was finally warm enough to be tolerable. Rachel dressed and tucked her gun into her belt again. She carried her computer, the hard drive and her Bible. Melea brought her own laptop. The other scientists were gathered around Mason. He was again focused on the bright red hot spot in the lower depths of the ruins. Rachel focused on Bryne as he began addressing the team.

"I had assumed Christobal was dead. I searched his apartment when I discovered the drill shaft had again been opened. He's been using crystalline cocaine since his arrival here. There's evidence he was sharing it with at least two others. I believe the two workers who have vanished were hiding him in the station and went into the ruins with him during the night. They've apparently found some way to generate heat in the ruins, and the level of heat could be detrimental to our station if it softens the ice between us and the ruins. We have to locate and turn off the heat source."

"What then?" Tolliver asked. "We don't have jail facilities here, McAllister. We have no way to know when the military will send us assistance."

123

"We have cryostasis facilities," Bryne replied grimly. "These men are clearly not rational, and we can't run the risk of having the generators stressed any further. When we capture them, we can freeze them until the military can take them back to the naval base. Such an action should have little impact on our continued work." He scanned the other male faces. "Does anyone have a better suggestion?"

"How do you propose we disable them?" Carson asked. "We aren't any match for those three physically."

"We have weapons they aren't privy to," Bryne replied. "And with twelve people, we have a superior force. We can have five teams of two and still leave two to stand guard here."

"We should search the station itself first," Carson warned. "They might still be up here."

"Set up the other four teams, Neill," said Bryne. "Melea and Mason can watch the drill shaft. If anyone finds a problem, pull the closest fire alarm and summon everyone else to that area. Rachel and I will start with the lab and storage closets."

"See that you don't remain there," Armand said suggestively. Bryne shot a killing glance at the Frenchman and then looked at Rachel.

"There's coffee and bread if you need something to eat before we go."

"I think I will get some," Rachel said. "Just give me a couple of minutes."

She went to the kitchen with her sleep deprived mind thinking obsessively about the glyph program diagramming a plan to live again. Bryne came into the kitchen and poured himself a cup of coffee. Instead of drinking it immediately, he put his hands on her shoulders. The familiar feeling of his warmth enveloped Rachel, and she leaned into his embrace.

"I need you to radio your father when we've searched this place from top to bottom. Tell him what's going on and ask him to get the base to send help. We don't have a good way to defend ourselves. I want you safely away from here as soon as possible."

She turned at the sound of his fear. He had not projected such an intense aura of fear even when they had left the dome to retrieve the containment cores. She put her hand on his face reassuringly. "God will take care of us, Bryne."

"I believe God helps those who help themselves," he said. "I won't feel calm until we have these three maniacs safely frozen."

The thought of cryogenic freezing suddenly struck Rachel as if it were a new concept. Her hand tightened over Bryne's arm as the aura she had first felt in Babel rose to towering heights in her mind. "I can believe Christobal is an evil man, but the other two seemed so normal. It's almost as if Babel has possessed them in some way. It feels... evil is the best description. It has since the moment I first saw it on the monitor."

"These people are crazy, Rachel. They would be crazy in any place and time. I should have known it during the trip in the crawler. It was obvious Christobal was unbalanced then." He pulled her closer. "I want you and Melea to stay locked in the generator room when I'm not with you. It can be locked down completely, and no one here has the ability to breech radiation safe walls. When the storm breaks, I want both of you safely away."

She thought to argue with him, but something told her he hadn't been able to abandon rational thought for the wild suppositions that were haunting her. She knew she wouldn't leave without him. If she were correct, no matter how absurb her thoughts might seem, they might be their only hope of escape.

"We'll stay in the generator room if we need to. In the meantime, we need to look for them in the station." She took his hand as they left the dining area. They walked through the corridors hurriedly and not talking. The storage closets appeared untouched, but they were full of equipment and took two hours to search them completely. The monotony made Rachel even sleepier; she began talking to stay focused.

"Are you sure all the others are with us?"

"They seem to be," he said slowly. "Of course, I never suspected the two construction workers. Have you seen anything that makes you worry?"

"Only Christobal," Rachel admitted. "If they aren't in the station, how long can they stay alive in the ruins?"

"I wouldn't have thought they could survive overnight." Bryne paused. "I keep wondering what else was on that hard drive he was studying. I wonder if the civilization gave him a share of their technology."

"It might have. Maybe we should look at it again."

"We probably should, but we need to search the ruins during daylight hours, and we only have about six hours to get it done. If we don't find them, we'll lock the shaft down and post armed guards. When that's done, we can look at the hard drive."

She felt a rush of fear and caught his hands. "Lock it down now, Bryne. It isn't worth the risk of going back into the ruins. If the hard drive gave them privileged information, they'll have a major advantage when you look for them. This place— It really is evil, Bryne. You can feel it. God didn't destroy people unless there was no hope for them."

"According to the Bible, God was very efficient when he destroyed civilizations, Rachel. If we've found the ruins of Sodom as we believe we have, there's scarcely anything left of it. I don't think any part of Babel survived except its artifacts." He smiled grimly. "I'm the team leader. I'm responsible for the lives of these people, and I can't lock them out of the dome when I know they'll die from that decision. It is, however, very heartwarming to know you care for my safety. I haven't had that security in a very long time." He pulled a delicate gold band from his pocket and slipped it on her hand.

"I bought this ring for Arielle, but she never saw it. She wouldn't talk about marriage because I couldn't promise her to believe in God and worship Him with her. When I knew she was gone, I felt as if God had punished me for my indecision, and I hated Him more than ever." He stopped speaking as he heard his own words. It wasn't possible to hate an entity that didn't exist. He accepted that he had always believed and hated himself for his belief.

He looked away from her as if to hide his emotions. "Do you know how my family died, Rachel? I know we live in a close knit profession, but it isn't really common knowledge. It isn't really fair for you to accept my proposal when you don't know about my mother."

"I read about it," Rachel admitted reluctantly. "Your mother was depressed after your father died."

"We lived in a coal mining town in Wales. All the men in my family had worked in the mine for generations. No one had ever gone beyond primary school, and most of them died from black lung by the time they were my age. I think because of that my father wanted me to be more. He was always reading and studying with me and my mother. We were a very close family, and we were happy. Then, my father was killed in a mine cave in. After he died, my mother spent all her time praying. I had always gone to church so I didn't see it as a sign of sickness." He sat down on one of the boxes. "One day she drove us to a cliff overlooking the sea and read the story of Jonah. Then she picked up my father's gun and looked at me. She said 'Jesus loves you, Bryne,' and she pulled the trigger. I don't remember anything for a while after that." His hand touched his chest involuntarily. "When I woke up, my sisters were dead. My mother was singing a hymn. It sounded normal until I looked at my little sisters and saw all the blood. I wanted to scream and cry, but I was quiet because I was afraid she would shoot me again if she knew I was still alive. I closed my eyes and prayed for it all to be a bad dream. I prayed until I heard her say, 'God help me.' I opened my eyes and saw her put the gun in her mouth. I can't forget what I saw then." His face contorted in the memory. "I was seven. I walked five miles to find help. I can't remember anything along the way except the pain and not being able to breathe. I didn't have the breath to cry. I also remember hating God every step of the way." She put fingers on his mouth to still the torrent of his pain.

"God heard your prayer, Bryne. You lived when you shouldn't have."

"I've argued that in my mind a million times. Still I come back to how can anyone believe God is good when He allowed someone to do what my mother did in His name? It took me twenty-five years not to dream about it. Every time I closed my eyes I heard my mother say, 'Jesus loves you, Bryne.'"

"Your mother was sick, Bryne," Rachel said gently. "She must have thought she would be rejoining your family with your father. She didn't know what she was doing." Rachel pulled him close and held him until she felt his body begin to relax. "Love is the greatest gift God gives us, Bryne. He brought us together so you could have that gift. You can't prove it, but I know you believe in how I love you. That's why faith is the evidence of things not seen. If you can believe I love you, then it's a small step to believe God brought the two of us together." She had been afraid her words wouldn't be right, but his expression told her that she had said what he needed to hear. He held her face in his hands and kissed her gently.

"You've made me believe it could be true, Rachel. That's a start, isn't it?"

"It's a good start. Just pray to know what to do. You'll begin to feel answers that couldn't have come from you." She would have said more but they heard Gibar calling them. Bryne took Rachel's hand and led her back to the kitchen. Gradually the other scientists and the four remaining construction workers returned. Each reported seeing nothing unusual.

"What about the heat source?" Bryne asked Mason.

"It's bigger. The temperature in the ruins is reading as ten below. It's increasing by ten degrees every twelve hours." He panned the screen. "I can't find anything else."

"We need to eat and get down there while the odds are twelve to three," Bryne said. "Let's get suited up. Rachel, you and Melea need to set up the generator room as a safe room."

"We'll set it up," Rachel agreed. "Then I'll work on the translation and try not to watch Mason's monitor." She released his hand and removed her cross to secure it around Bryne's neck. When he reached up to stop her, she caught his fingers. "Let me. Please, let me."

He stood very still while she fastened the cross. When it was secured, he tucked it into his shirt. "There are those that would expect this to burn me as it did Bram Stoker's Dracula."

"No. You just want people to think that." She tucked the cross in more securely and kissed the hollow of his throat over it. "Hurry back, Bryne."

She couldn't watch the men begin rappelling down the shaft. When they were down, she asked Mason to pray with her. She moved food, water and waste receptacles into the generator room.

Then she set up her computer where she could watch Mason recording what was being seen in the ruins. The team moved rapidly through the public buildings and to the end of the main street. Rachel didn't know Bryne's transmitter was the one being recorded. His sense of direction was better than that of the other scientists and took him rapidly toward the hot spot.

The screen took Mason, Rachel and Melea into a large building in better condition than the others. The street level floor was almost empty, but a smooth stone staircase was at the back and led up and down. The screen took them down first. There was a deep darkness until a bright light came from behind the transmitter and illuminated a scene from hell. Frozen skeletons were fastened to the stone walls. On the floor was a pile of similar skeletons. The area had obviously been a holding cell at one time. Fragmented metal bars were on the floor. On the walls were a series of repeating glyphs in reddish brown residue.

"Oh," Rachel whispered. "It's written in blood, Mason. Freeze that and transfer it to my computer."

Mason transferred the image and then returned to the live feed. Bryne made his way around the edge of the room and then descended another series of stairs to a medical laboratory area. A body was strapped to a table. Several skeletons lay on the floor near the table.

"He's directly over the hot spot," Mason said frantically. "Feed three, this is Mason. Return to the street level. You're over the hot spot. Rachel, who's feed three?"

The feed stopped, and they all froze until a burst of light came from behind the transmitter for a second time. The screen revealed a different reddish glow. They could all see an ancient generator that was obviously working at full capacity.

Feed three's voice came to them through a blanket of static. The accent was unmistakably English. "It looks as if they've tapped into the volcano for heat. This generator seems to be built over a vent. The metal alloy must be one we've never seen because the heat it's containing is incredible.

"Feed three is Bryne," Melea said.

"Bryne, get out of there," Rachel demanded. She felt as if her heart were in her throat smothering her. "Christobal and the others might be there." He showed no signs of hearing her, and she was ready to run from the room to rescue him. At the same time, she couldn't tear her eyes away from the screen.

The next flight of stairs stopped on a long corridor lined with cubicles. Each had a doorway made of metal with a number of gages on it. Several of them were ajar. The first door on the right was ajar, and Bryne opened it further. Inside the walls were covered with ice. On the floor was a layer of ice with a body lying on it.

"These appear to be cryogenic chambers," Bryne said. "It looks as if they tried to freeze themselves in the hope of outlasting the destruction." Bryne bent over the body to examine it. "This chamber must have been breached soon after it was sealed. This body isn't as decomposed as the others. It has a layer of moisture on the skin that I wouldn't expect. It's almost jelly like." He touched the shiny wet surface and then looked at the thermometer he was carrying. "It's two below zero on the Fahrenheit scale now. This has to be your hot spot, Mason."

He heard or felt the footsteps coming from behind him. Mason and Rachel saw the screen spin wildly to reveal a wild faced man who had been one of their construction crew. He was holding a club above his head. Bryne lost his footing on the ice and fell back. The screen went dead as Rachel screamed a warning she thought Bryne couldn't possibly hear. She was running toward the drill shaft when Melea restrained her.

Bryne's actions were automatic. He pulled the gun from his belt and fired at his attacker aiming to kill. The worker fell on his legs but Bryne managed to scramble away just as Braden ran into the cubicle. He fired again and as Braden fell, he scrambled to his feet and ran up the stairs. He heard his own voice say, "God help me," as he reached with street. His transmitter and all the others were broadcasting Rachel's frantic call.

"He's all right," Dr. Carson said. "What did you see, Bryne?"

"They were down there," Bryne panted. He was as stunned by his spontaneous prayer as he was by the attack. "I didn't see Christobal, but the other two attacked me."

"Show us," Carson ordered him.

The team returned to the lower level as a group, but Rachel couldn't watch. She was trying to translate the blood written glyphs when she heard Melea gasp.

"They're cryogenic chambers, Rachel," Melea said. "Look." They gathered around the screen and saw the contents of an intact chamber. A frozen intact humanoid was inside. It looked as if it might awaken at any moment. The door had the glyph, to live again, on it.

The team members moved away to the open chamber and collected the bodies of the two workers. Gibar and Carson bent over the ice mummy and examined it. The face, though contracted, seemed to be smiling.

"Get out," Rachel whispered. "Please, God, get them out." She had never felt such an oppressive sense of evil. As the screen dimmed again, she moved back and read the words written in blood. "From the depths of our despair, we cry out to the God of heaven."

CHAPTER 11

"We couldn't find Christobal," Gibar said. Even the unflappable Russian was wide eyed as the search party climbed out of the drill shaft. "He has to be down there. The workers weren't even wearing coats." He held up a metallic vest. "They were both wearing these. They're still warm. They must be some sort of personal heat generators.

Bryne was silent as he emerged from the ruins. His emotions showed in how he sealed the drill shaft. He brought strips of metal and fastened them to the floor until no single man could have reopened it. When he came out of the drill room, he locked the door behind him.

Rachel met him at the door and put her arms around his waist ignoring the knowing glances. Bryne's face was very pale, and he didn't speak as he moved past the team, but he returned the embrace with emotions she could feel. The remaining team members gathered around him.

"We have to get out of here tomorrow. We can't risk looking for the others any longer. If anyone disagrees, I'll be happy to turn the project over to them." Everyone looked relieved and nodded assent as Bryne continued. "Secure your quarters carefully tonight then. Mason, could we see you for just a minute?"

Mason followed them to Bryne's quarters. When the door was secured, Bryne said, "I want to marry Rachel. She said you're a minister, Mason. Can you legally marry us?" He looked at Rachel as if asking for her affirmation.

A particle stream of thoughts raced through her mind. She felt committed to Bryne but hadn't really expected his desperate effort to finalize their commitment. She thought of what everyone would say on knowing how quickly they had come to their decision. She thought of her father's reaction. Nothing else outweighed her desire to be with Bryne.

"Will you marry us, Mason?" she asked without taking her eyes from Bryne.

"We'll have to make up a document in lieu of a license." Mason said. "May I use your computer, Bryne?"

"I'll thank you to use it." Bryne stripped off his parka and dropped it on the floor. He was stripping off his bib and the second layer of clothes over his wet suit. Rachel's cross was easily visible on his wet suit, and Bryne closed his hand over it. He spoke to Rachel as if they were still alone.

"Could you see what happened down there?"

"I was praying you would get back," Rachel said.

"It felt like I was running from a crypt. When I was running up the stairs, I realized I was praying to get back to you. I can't recall having ever felt that way—"

"I need your full name, Dr. McAllister," Mason said.

"Bryne Jacob McAllister," Bryne said. "I'm a British citizen. Date of birth July 29, 1968."

"Rachel Leah Madison," Rachel said. "I'm a United States citizen. Date of birth June 11, 1980."

"OK," Mason said. "You'll need a witness."

"Get Melea," Bryne said. "I'll get changed."

Melea persuaded them to marry in the dining room with everyone witnessing the ceremony. Bryne wanted no one else in attendance but conceded to observers so there could be no questions about his relationship with Rachel. The bride wore the only dress she had brought. It was emerald silk. Mason said the ceremony without need for a prayer book quoting the passage from the Book of Ruth.

"Where you go, I will go. Where you live, I will live. Your people will be my people. Your God will be my God. Where you die, I will die and there will I be buried. The Lord do so to me and more also if anything but death should part us." He looked at Bryne. "Repeat after me, Bryne. I, Bryne, take you Rachel to be

134

my lawfully wedded wife." Bryne repeated the vows with his eyes never leaving Rachel's face. "To have and to hold from this day forward, for better for worse, for richer for poorer, in sickness and in health for as long as we both shall live."

Rachel couldn't stop smiling as she repeated the vows. In the midst of chaos, she felt serene. She could forget everything except Bryne's eyes. She heard Mason pronounce them man and wife, and then she was enveloped in her husband's arms.

Melea broke open a bottle of champagne and turned on blaring Greek music. They ended up dancing a Greek marriage dance and spreading around the meals they had broken open for supper. Bryne was collecting the marriage document Mason had created when Neill Carson pulled him aside. Carson's face was flushed, and his eyes seemed unusually bright.

"So you'll have her one way or another, Bryne. I didn't know how far you'd be willing to go to win our bet."

Bryne's face flushed at the slur. "It isn't like that, Neill. You should remember I conceded that bet. I shouldn't have made it in the first place. I have been interested only in a long term relationship with Rachel from the moment I met her."

"As you've often said, you know how to get what you want." Carson laughed derisively as he walked away. Mason restrained Bryne from following him.

"Walk away, Dr. McAllister. What he said is only words, and saying them doesn't make them the truth. Time will prove what your feelings are."

"He calls himself a good, God fearing Christian," Bryne muttered. "How can you believe when your world is as full of hypocrites as my own?" His words weren't arrogant at all at that moment, but they were evidence of his ongoing struggle with faith.

"Faith is very personal," Mason said. "Mine wasn't personal or strong until I lost my firstborn son. I left my church because I couldn't understand why God didn't save my child when He must have heard me begging Him. Finally, when I could think rationally, I knew He let His own son die for my sake. He couldn't stop that evil without sacrificing the rest of us. Then I knew He was crying with me. The way other people live isn't our business. Faith and living in faith has to be between you and God if it's to be real."

"Your son is still dead," Bryne said.

"Only in this life. My son is in heaven, and I'll see him again. That time will last forever." Mason was physically a diminutive man, but his face radiated a confident strength that Bryne felt was almost supernatural. He had seen that same aura in Melea, Arielle and Rachel. He wondered what it felt like to believe in something on such a basis that proof was superfluous. He was reflecting on that thought when Rachel put a scarf around his neck as if she were a Greek bride.

"Come away with me," she whispered. She caught his hands and pulled him toward the corridor. When they were away from the others she put a slip of paper in his hands. It was inscribed with the hieroglyphics for a joining of Osiris and Isis. Bryne read them with a surge of joy that made him forget Dr. Carson's words.

"You didn't word your note right," she smiled.

"You'll have a lifetime to teach me, Rachel."

Her hands on his body seemed able to warm him through the barrier of clothing. She pressed him against the corridor wall and let her fingers unbutton his shirt until they could slide under his knit undershirt. She was kissing him as her hands caressed his chest. Her touch was more exciting than any woman's touch had ever been to Bryne. He pulled her tightly into his arms. His mouth made her ache to have him as close as he could be.

"I've been taking the pills you gave me," she whispered. "Come with me and let me be your wife."

"I love you, Rachel," he said. "I love you so much." He carried her into his quarters. When they were inside, Rachel locked the door and pulled him close. His hands ran through her hair slowly. The thick curly mass fell over her shoulders. As his hands slid over the tangled curls, they took off her jacket. His thumbs caressed her cheeks and stopped at the corners of her mouth to shape it to his own. She could feel every muscle in his chest and even his heartbeat through their clothes. As her desire grew, she pulled at his clothing until she could free it from his body and caress his bare skin with her lips and hands. The sensation of his skin against hers was almost unbearable. She couldn't remember how they made it to the bed when her legs felt weak. Rachel felt as if she couldn't get Bryne close enough until the moment

136

when their bodies became one. She could feel the cross pressed between them and then sensation overwhelmed everything else. The emotions of making love to his wife defined fulfillment for Bryne. He had never felt physically and emotionally satiated until that moment.

"There has to be a God because only God could have made you," he whispered.

"God brought us together. You know He did in your heart." Rachel rested her face against his chest feeling warm as she hadn't been since their arrival on the seventh continent. He had to think of what to say, and it felt awkward.

"I hope the passage I chose was all right. I'm not a great Biblical scholar, but I always liked that vow."

"It was what I'd always wanted read at my wedding. I don't think you just guessed that." She closed her eyes and he felt her drift off to sleep.

Sleep was impossible for Bryne. As she lay vulnerable in his arms, Bryne felt a growing fear that was so intense, it wiped away every other feeling within him. It was a completely unexpected feeling. He had expected making love to Rachel would possess him completely and knew it couldn't because he could so easily lose that moment. He had never been in a situation where he felt so threatened by forces he couldn't explain, and he spent their wedding night trying to plan for their escape the following day. He approached the problem as a scientist, but the solution was not forth-coming.

In the compartment around the drill shaft, the strips of steel slowly began to peel away from the floor. They popped off like rubber bands, one by one. The rubber sealed port glowed red as it moved slowly up and then out of the shaft.

Rachel awakened suddenly. She was alone in the bed and cold despite the covers. She was shivering as she sat up and scanned the room for Bryne. He was on the floor with the radio trying to make contact with the world outside of their station. His expression told her he was having problems.

"What's wrong?" she asked him.

"I can't get a signal lock. With this type of radio, that shouldn't be possible." He looked up at her and saw she was unnerved. "I'm no radio technician. That concept always eluded me." She knew he was lying to her to hide his fear of being trapped in Erebus station.

"Come back to bed, Bryne. It's probably just a storm blocking the signal. You can try later, and I'm freezing to death now." He came back to bed in response to her statement and slipped under the covers to pull her close. She relaxed as his warmth enveloped her.

"I don't think many men ever appreciate how wonderful it is to awaken beside the woman you love," he said. Her hands slipped under his clothes easily. He pulled her close until she could feel every breath he drew as if it were her own. Later, she found herself looking at the terrible scar that was wrapped around the left side of his chest. Time had faded it so she hadn't noticed it until that moment. She traced it with her fingers.

"Is this where you were shot?"

"Right here," he said and pointed to an area just above his heart. "When I was nineteen I went to the hospital in Liston and tried to view the records. They had been destroyed because so many years had passed, but I found the doctor who performed the surgery. He told me I should have died. I wondered why I was spared for a life of isolation. There isn't any accomplishment that takes away that emptiness. After all those years, I think you've brought me the answer." Bryne caressed Rachel's hair.

"I remember feeling unbearably alone three times in my life. The first was when I woke up in hospital with all the tubes and in so much pain. I was alone. Everyone was dead. I cried, and they sent the psychiatrists to talk to me. What I needed was someone to hold me, but no one did. I think people were afraid to be close to a child whose mother had done such an evil thing. It marked me all through my childhood. It didn't take long to learn that showing emotion would only summon more psychiatrists.

"The other two times was when I graduated Oxford with my first degree and when I stood on the podium to receive the Nobel Prize. I was the only one there who had no one to rejoice with them. There were people who had come with me to Sweden from Oxford, but no one who really cared for my sake."

"How did you get by?" Rachel asked.

"I imagined my father being there." He smiled at her expression. "Yes, I supposed everyone has moments where they believe in things that aren't seen. Imagining my father carried me through some terrible moments." He caressed her face. "Actually there was a fourth time. It was three nights ago when I thought you wouldn't ever care for me. It was the worst night of my life. I was thinking some terrible thoughts. Melea came and told me I should pray. She said, 'Haven't you ever just found yourself saying please and not knowing who you're asking for help?' When you slept in my arms in the generator room, I found myself doing just that."

"You won't ever be alone again," she promised him. "I'll be beside you all my life. Did you know Jacob was married to Rachel in the Bible?"

"I hope you can be happy being the Rachel who's married to Bryne. My father's name was Jacob, and it doesn't really feel like my name to me. Of course, Melea frequently calls me Bryne Jacob when I'm getting a lecture."

"I hadn't ever heard the name, Bryne, before you." She stretched out on his body and looked down into his eyes. "That's fitting since I've never known anyone like you."

"It's the Welch version of Bryan," he said. "Even the Brits have some trouble with it. Have you ever been to London?"

"For about a week when I was in college," she told him. "I was thrown out of the British Museum at closing time because I couldn't tear myself away from the Egyptian collection."

"I practically lived there when I was in the university. I was a soccer player then. Did you know?"

"You were on the 1992 Olympic team."

"Very good. You did your research just as I did mine. We didn't medal, but we put up a good fight. I ran all the time then to train. It was about five kilometers from my flat to the museum."

"How did you get so good at soccer?"

"I started playing in the orphanage. I was understandably having problems dealing with my anger, and I wasn't brawny enough to survive rugby. It's still quite a rush to kick things around, you know. My first team was the Liston Lynxes. I was number fourteen.

139

That's one of the codes I use to secure data even now. Ninety-two for the Olympiad, fourteen for my number and Lynx.

"I was studying geology then. My father died because a minor earthquake caused the coal mine where he worked to cave in. I always said I'd find a way to warn people so no one would ever die from an earthquake again. It helped me to be at peace with his death. Afterwards, geology just lost its pull on me. I had always been a student of ancient history, and I knew my geological skills would only facilitate this work. That's the story of the transition from geology to archeology."

"Did you ever think that you might have been a coal miner too if your father hadn't died?" she asked him.

"I don't suppose I wanted to think that way, but I have. I've asked myself would he have died to save other people? No question. He would have. He actually died trying to save another man. So though I've regretted losing him most of my life, I think he would have died to keep me from being a coal miner and losing my life slowly from the work. When I developed the earthquake technology, I did it for him. No one else knew that or cared, but it was important to me." He touched her face.

"This morning when I was watching you sleep, I thought I wouldn't have ever known you if Arielle had lived. Just having that thought should tell you how much I love you."

"There's a verse in the Bible in Romans that says "'all things work together for the good of them that love God and are called according to his purpose.'"

"That would have to apply to you." He kissed her forehead. "I'll try to make it apply to me as well. I'm ready to take you home, Rachel."

"Where's your house?" she asked. "Or do you have a house?"

"In Kensington," he said. "That's between London proper and the Notting Hill district. It's sort of a townhouse. Three floors straight up, not counting the cellar. It was built in the late 1800's, and I bought it fully furnished from the estate of an unmarried teacher at Cambridge. Of course, I haven't done very much with it. There are piles of books everywhere. If not for the housekeeper, it would probably be uninhabitable. Could you live in London, Rachel? I wouldn't want to deprive you of your father's company, but the university does pay me quite well. I'm very certain they'd hire you."

"I could live anywhere you were." She smiled into his eyes. "Our life together is more important than anything else now. I could just stay here and let you hold me forever."

He held her very close then and when she was almost asleep she heard him say, "Contentment was always just a word. I never knew what it would feel like until now."

Hunger drove them out of bed and into the shower just before ten o'clock. Standing under the water, Rachel kept spontaneously embracing Bryne who couldn't stop smiling.

"Tell me why you gave me your cross," he asked.

"Two reasons. I wanted to let everyone see you're mine, and I wanted to remind you that you belong to me and God. When we get home I want to get you a wedding ring. I wish I could get you one just like this one."

"I have a good friend in Egypt," he said. "We could go there. I'll be happy to wear anything you get me, but you needn't worry that I'll ever forget where I belong. There won't be anyone else, Rachel. You're everything I need." He pulled her close. "I want to take you all over the world and show you all the things I've seen and wished I could see them with someone I loved. We'll take all the data with us and write it up while we travel." He held her face in his hands. "You aren't still feeling guilty because of Gary, are you? I wouldn't want us to have that shadow over our marriage."

"I prayed to know what to do," she told him fervently. "God sent me to you, Bryne. There were too many things neither of us could explain otherwise. You're my soul mate, and I'm yours. I believe that's for this life and the next life."

"It's as if a switch has been flipped and suddenly I have everything I've wanted and needed all my life. I love you, Rachel."

His words and his arms were wound tightly around her when she realized the great depths of feeling in being a part of him. She would have been content lying in his arms all day.

"Let's just stay here, Bryne. I have some almonds and a package of dried fruit in my suitcase. We've got water. We have each other. Let's just stay here and hold each other."

"I wish we could, but we need to leave, Rachel." His face was suddenly serious. "I've never been so happy or so very afraid. This place has an aura of— I can't describe it, but I have to take you away from here. If you'll excuse my inexplicable devotion to intuition on this occasion, I'll try not to subject you to it again."

"I know what you're feeling because I'm feeling it, too." She turned off the shower and handed him a towel. "Let's find a way to get out of here."

They were drying each other when the knocking began. They could hear it up and down the corridor. When it came to their door, Bryne reached across Rachel to pick up his gun. He pulled on his clothes hurriedly as the knocking continued. Rachel followed suit though she struggled with her buttons because she was trembling. Bryne gave her the gun as if on second thought as he went to the door.

"Who is it?" he demanded.

"Gibar," said a faint voice. "There's a problem at the drill shaft."

"What sort of problem?" Bryne asked as he opened the door. He had seconds to recognize Christobal's face but not enough time to avoid the first blow of the staff Christobal was wielding. Bryne staggered back as his right ribs cracked from the force of the blow. He was struggling to breathe when the staff swept his legs.

Rachel screamed and kept screaming as she struggled to take the safety off the gun. Christobal started toward her at that moment. His expression froze her in sheer terror. She saw Bryne scramble to his feet, and he ran to put himself between her and Christobal. He struck his opponent twice, driving him into the corridor. As he braced himself for Christobal's next attack, Bryne glanced back to make certain Rachel was out of the way. Christobal took that second of diverted attention and used it to his advantage. He swung the heavy staff with all his strength and struck Bryne across the forehead. The force of the blow was so great that Bryne was lifted off his feet and thrown into the wall. He slid to the floor not moving or breathing.

Christobal smiled as he looked at Rachel. He spoke to her in the ancient tongue of the computer hard drive. Rachel raised the gun with rage for her husband and fired four times directly into

Christobal's chest. She never felt a second's remorse as her enemy fell dead at her feet. She felt for his pulse and then climbed over his body to reach Bryne.

Bryne didn't respond to being turned and shaken. He didn't respond when she screamed his name. For a terrible moment, she thought he was dead. She was praying aloud when she saw and felt him draw a shallow breath. She screamed for help again and carefully held his head so his airway was open. The blood from the wound on his head ran over her hands.

Slowly the others appeared looking restless despite the late hour. Carson and Marquette went to check the drill shaft, which had been resealed. Mason, Gibar and Tolliver carried Bryne to the laboratory and put him on the stretcher. Rachel followed praying they would be able to do something to save his life. Civilization had never seemed so far away. Outside another storm began as if to put them at the mercy of Babel.

CHAPTER 12

"Shouldn't he be coming around?" Mason asked. "He's been out for more than fifteen minutes."

"Scan him," Tolliver suggested. "He could have a hemorrhage." When the others hesitated, he pulled the crescent shaped PET scanner from the ceiling and positioned it over Bryne's head. The image appeared on the computer screen in the control panel.

"He's bleeding in his posterior fossa," Tolliver said as he outlined an increasingly dark area inside the back of Bryne's skull. "If we don't stop the bleeding, he'll herniate his brain stem from the pressure. That would assure his death. The medical computer has a protocol for performing a burr hole procedure. Start an intravenous line, Melea. Turn him over and get the laser attachment. We need to perform the burr hole to release the pressure. That's the best we can give him." He was so confident that Rachel and the others felt comfortable leaving Bryne to his expertise. They never thought that his medical training was no better than their own.

"Pray," Rachel begged everyone. "Pray for him."

"Should we offer a sacrifice as well?" Carson commented. Gibar laughed heartily as if the comment was incongruously funny. Rachel was too shocked to respond. She had never seen Neill Carson behave inappropriately. She held onto Bryne's hand and prayed.

When the procedure was underway, Mason prayed with Rachel while Melea injected a clot producing drug. Tolliver used the computer to target the pocket of blood and produce the modern day equivalent of a burr hole. When the resultant blood flow slowed to a trickle, he reversed the laser attachment and sealed Bryne's skin. Melea used a whole body tomography machine to scan Bryne for other injuries.

"He has two broken ribs and a small hemorrhage in his chest," she told Rachel. "There's some cartilage damage in his left knee. That's it. Nothing else life threatening." She repeated the PET scan on Bryne's brain. "The bulk of the clot is gone, Rachel."

"Why isn't he waking up?" Rachel asked. Bryne's hand felt lifeless between her hands.

"It's a bad injury, Rachel," Tolliver said nonchalantly. "If we didn't have state of the art equipment, he would have died from it. He still might. I'm certain he has some swelling of his brain tissue. I'll get on the radio and send for help. We need to get out of here. Surely they'll evacuate us now."

"Wait here for just a minute," Rachel pleaded. "I need to go to my quarters."

She ran through the corridors, hurdling Christobal's corpse to gather their computers, the radio and the bottles of medicine. She also located Bryne's gun on the floor. She put everything into Bryne's duffel bag and hurried back to the laboratory area with her gun in her free hand. She hid it under her clothes before reentering the laboratory. When Tolliver left, she locked the door behind him.

"What's going on, Rachel?" Mason asked. "I'm not a scientist, but I can tell you at least two of our coworkers are losing touch with reality. I couldn't believe what they said."

"This place is doing something to them. First Christobal, Braden and Wright," Rachel said. "Now the others are starting to act like strangers. Everything the people of Babel left behind says they had plans to live again. Before I killed Christobal, he spoke to me in the language of Babel."

"They tried to freeze themselves," Mason said. "It didn't work. How could that affect us now?"

"Did you see the other workmen this morning?" she asked him. His expression answered her. "They must be down below, Mason. I don't know how Babel has affected them, but I know they couldn't survive down there if it hadn't changed them in some way." She pulled out the radio. "Find some way to lock onto a satellite or wire this to your computer and send a message they can't block. Bryne couldn't get a satellite lock this morning."

"Maybe I can attach it to a laser," Mason said. "God will lead us out of here."

She believed Mason in her heart, but she was in a survival mode at that moment. Rational thought wouldn't come. As she sat beside Bryne for an endless stretch of time. She couldn't do anything except pray he would survive. Melea repeated the scan on Bryne's brain hourly, and it confirmed the bleeding was controlled. Half the day passed before they realized none of the other team members had come to check their leader's progress. It was an ominous confirmation of their previous observations.

Rachel was dozing with her head resting on the edge of the stretcher when she felt Bryne move. A quick glance at her watch told her it was three o'clock, six hours since his injury. He groaned, a deep, haunting sound of his pain. Rachel grasped his hand and leaned over him.

"Bryne, can you hear me," she asked.

"Rachel." He opened his eyes and looked past her and then all around the room. "Rachel?" Her name was spoken as a frantic plea. When he tried to sit up, she held his shoulders.

"Don't move, Bryne. Christobal hit you in the head. It caused a hemorrhage. Tolliver had to do a burr hole with the laser. Do you understand?"

"I understand." He relaxed under her hands. "Did you get Christobal?"

"He's dead," she reassured him. She felt a tremendous relief at hearing his coherent voice. She had feared he had suffered some irreparable brain damage from the blow and the bleeding. "Mason is trying to get help on the radio."

"My head hurts," Bryne said. "It's very intense. I may need something for the pain. Please uncover my eyes. I panicked when I couldn't see you."

Rachel felt her heart turn over in her chest, but she kept Bryne from touching his face. She didn't want him to know his eyes were uncovered.

"I'm afraid to touch the bandages just now, Bryne. Please hold my hand and lie still. I've been praying for you to wake up for six hours."

147

"I'll be still if you give me something for the pain. I've never liked seeing people writhe, and I don't want to try it myself." He shifted positions and gasped as his chest stabbed him. His hands tightened on Rachel's hand and the edge of the bed. Melea inserted a needle into the intravenous line and injected five milligrams of synthetic morphine. Bryne relaxed visibly after several seconds.

"It's better now. I felt like I couldn't breathe. My chest was on fire." He closed his eyes. "Tell Mason to try an infrared beam with a radio wave attached. That should be outside of blocking frequencies."

"You need to take your pills, Bryne," she urged him.

"Did you take yours?" he asked. "I think we both know you've been fully exposed now."

"I took mine." She kissed his hand and then put the pills in his mouth and put a straw between his lips. He swallowed the anti viral medication without difficulty.

"I can't think right now, Rachel. You'll have to think for me."

"I'll take care of you," Rachel vowed. "Just sleep." She looked at Melea who gave another five milligrams of morphine. That increment was enough to put Bryne to sleep.

Melea pulled the scanner down again and typed a different command into the computer. Then they could see what none of them had seen earlier. The area around his optic nerves was pale, which indicated a critical loss of blood supply.

"His optic nerves are damaged," Melea said in horror. "He's blind, Rachel."

Tears ran down Rachel's face as she touched the terrible bruise on Bryne's forehead. "How could it have happened? It was blunt trauma to the front of his head. Can't his vision still come back?" Guilt swept over her and she thought of all the things she should have done. If she had shot Christobal sooner, he might not have delivered the final blow. She could see herself standing frozen in shock as Bryne battled to protect her. "We can't let him know."

"He's strong," Melea asserted. "He isn't the sort of man to just give up."

"I've got a satellite lock," Macon said. "The infrared beacon went through. What frequency should I use?"

Rachel moved to his side and put in her father's frequency. When his voice came over the speaker, she breathed a sigh of relief. "Rachel, what's happening there? The storm front has cleared but no one has been able to raise you on the radio. The base called me." The comment told all of them that Tolliver had not tried to contact the base.

"We need help, Dad," Rachel said. "The ruins here are technologically advanced. From what we've translated, they appear to be the ruins of Babel. They've left glyphs throughout the ruins saying they're going to live again. Dr. Christobal went into the ruins several nights ago, and he didn't come back up until today. He was able to live down there without protective clothing. He took two of the construction workers with him, and yesterday they attacked the other scientists when they were in the ruins. Christobal came up during the night and tried to kill Bryne. I shot him, but Bryne was seriously injured. Now the other construction workers have disappeared. We've been trying to contact you, but something is blocking the radio signals. We can't reach the base either. Mason thought of attaching the radio waves to an infrared beam or we'd still be in radio silence."

"Are you saying there's something in the ruins that's able to take over people's minds?" the colonel asked incredulously. "Rachel, that's a little farfetched."

"I know it is, Dad, but I promise it's the truth. There's a hot spot in the ruins from a generator powered by a volcanic vent. Look at it with a satellite."

"I will," the colonel assured her. "I'm going to ask the base to evacuate everyone at Erebus station until we have more information. Keep the radio on, and I'll let you know when we have it set up. Can you transmit any of your data?"

Rachel looked at Mason who nodded. "We'll send you everything we have, Dad. Hurry please."

"I will."

Rachel gave the microphone to Mason, and he plugged it into his computer and began transmitting everything he had filmed to the colonel's computer. Ten minutes later, he signed off.

"We need to get some food," Melea said. "And water."

"I'll go," said Rachel. "I have a gun, and I'll use it on anybody who tries to stop me." She emptied the duffel bag and shouldered it. "Lock the doors while I'm gone."

Rachel was praying for safe passage while she walked down the corridor. The station was silent, and she didn't encounter anyone. The area around the drill shaft was brightly lit, but Rachel didn't try to look into it. In the kitchen, she loaded the bag with food and filled a tank with potable water. She was on her way back when Dr. Carson stepped in front of her. She hadn't heard him or seen him until he appeared. His eyes were luminous, and he looked much younger.

"You know what's happening, don't you, Rachel?"

"I know all of you are acting in a way I can't explain," she stammered. "I need to get back to Bryne, Neill. Let me pass."

"We belong to a different team now, Rachel. Babel has given us a very special gift. When we spread it over the earth, we'll be world rulers. We'll be gods." His words were a confirmation of what she had suggested to Bryne, but even as she realized they were true, the truth became overwhelming.

"I can't think right now, Neill," she said. "I need to get back to Bryne. When you know more, come to the infirmary and tell all of us."

"You'll know more very soon." He stroked her arm with his sweaty palm. The cold damp sensation made Rachel recoil involuntarily. "Your loyalties are misguided, Rachel. Before you waste your life with Bryne McAllister, you need to know who you've married. He chose you as a sexual conquest. Before he left Houston, he wagered he would get you in bed. He was very successful. Your international marriage is only legal if no one contests it. You should contest it or better still let him die. He won't have a life as a blind man."

Neill's words made her shudder. She also had the impression his accusations about Bryne were true and couldn't bear to believe it. She edged her way around her chairman and moved toward the laboratory. "I don't care, Neill. I love him. Nothing could change that."

She could feel his eyes on her all the way to the door. His accusations took on a life of their own even when the secured door separated them. She walked to the microbiology station and swabbed her hand and arm as if she had become a specimen to be analyzed.

"What are you doing?" Mason asked.

"Neill touched me. His hands were wet." She flipped on the electron microscope. While it was calibrating, she made a slide from the swab and inserted it into the machine. A viral structure appeared almost immediately.

"That looks like Ebola," Melea said in horror.

Rachel scrubbed her hands and arm with disinfectant. Then she typed into the computer the command to categorize the virus and its genetic material.

"They were working on one of the bodies, weren't they?" she asked Melea.

"Tolliver and Marquette put two in the freezer."

Rachel gloved her hands and went into the freezer to take swabs from both. The body from the cryogenic chamber had the same virus on its skin.

She scrubbed again and turned on her computer returning to the medical document she had found earlier. Using a translation interface, she plugged in the linguistic symbol for virus in every language she could recall. A glyph appeared on her screen. She shuddered when she saw it was similar to the glyph, to live again.

"They left the virus in the cryogenic chambers," she said slowly. "It must be carrying some sort of genetic code that can change our DNA." Her face paled. "Bryne was down there. Why wasn't he affected?" The words were scarcely off her lips when she realized Bryne had been taking anti viral drugs throughout their stay in the dome.

"Do either of you take any medicine?" she asked Mason and Melea.

"I'm on blood pressure medicine," Melea said. "Why, Rachel?"

"Bryne has a virus. He's been on anti viral therapy, and he gave the same drugs to me so I wouldn't contract it from him. That may be why he didn't contract the virus when he went in the cryogenic chamber. I think we should all take it."

"I'm ready," Mason asserted. "I'll pour the water. You bring the pills."

She gave each of them a dose and then returned to her computer. Melea warmed the food, and they ate mechanically. Bryne awakened as they were clearing the leftovers.

"Rachel," he said hoarsely. "Where are you?"

"I'm right here," she said as she took his hand. As she touched him, Neill's accusation came flooding back into her mind. "I've been watching over you. Do you need something else for the pain?"

"Not yet." He tried to sit up and barely suppressed his response to the discomfort. Melea brought an anesthetic patch and applied it to his chest over the broken ribs.

"That will help in a little while, Bryne," Melea assured him.

"I need to be able to see you, Rachel," he pleaded as he lay back. "Please take the covering off my eyes."

Rachel knew he would have to know the truth sooner or later, and Melea's hand on her shoulder encouraged her to tell him.

"There isn't any covering, Bryne," she said. She took his hand and guided it to his face. "The bleeding damaged your optic nerves."

As his hand groped his face, Bryne's expression became one of complete terror and disbelief. He jerked his hand away from her grasp and held his hands in front of his eyes.

"I can't see at all," he said. "I'm blind."

In that moment, Rachel could feel her husband's thoughts as if they were her own. He had feared dependence on others all his life. Blindness was not a surmountable obstacle for him. It represented accepting a lifestyle he considered worse than death.

"It can't be permanent," she insisted desperately. "It's just from the bleeding. We're getting out of here, Bryne. We were able to contact my father. He's going to send help. We can get you back to doctors who know what to do."

"What kind of scan did you run?" he demanded as if he hadn't heard her. "What did it show?"

"It was a PET scan," Rachel said.

"And the nerves were pale? Tell me, Rachel. Were they pale?"

"They were paler than the rest, Bryne." She wasn't ready for his reaction. He came off the table and yanked the intravenous

152

line out of his arm. He scrambled across the floor until he hit the cabinets leaving a trail of blood behind him. He was in the medical equipment feeling for the scalpels before they realized what he was doing. He was poised to slash his own throat when Rachel caught his arm. She had to use all her strength to fight for her husband's life in the moments that followed. She believed only God could have given her the power to restrain his arm until Mason came to her aid. Mason finally pinned Bryne to the ground and held him with difficulty while Melea drew up a sedative with unsteady hands.

They had to hold him down for five minutes before the sedative began taking effect. Only then could they apply pressure to the bleeding wound the intravenous line had produced. When Bryne was on the stretcher, Mason fastened the restraints around his legs and moved to bind his arms. Bryne lay very still except for one hand that reached up to yank the cross free from his neck. He threw it across the room and then lay still as Mason restrained his arms.

"If you love me, Rachel," Bryne said, "you'll kill me or give me the gun and let me do it myself. I can't live this way. I won't."

"I do love you, Bryne," she whispered. "If it could be me, I'd give up my sight for you right now. If you love me, if you were speaking the truth when you said you loved me, then you have to live for me because I need you." Her tears fell on his hand as she pressed her face against it. "I need you so much. Please don't leave me."

He cried then like a child with his body shaking from the effort of crying. "What good will I be to you or anyone else? How can you love a man you'll pity for the rest of your life? Rachel held him until the sedative made him sleep, but she knew he didn't want her embrace. It was as if he were a stranger. She sat back numbly when she released him. Mason found the cross and brought it to her.

"He can't help but be afraid, Rachel," Mason said. "He's scared. I would be, too. If anything, the world is more visually oriented now than it ever has been."

"I know," Rachel said mechanically. "We've got to make him believe there's a chance..." The knock on the laboratory door froze her.

Melea went to the door. "Who is it?"

"It's Tolliver." The answer was terse. "Let me in."

Mason hid the radio and the anti viral drugs. Melea opened the door while Rachel kept the gun held ready under her jacket. Tolliver seemed completely normal.

"How's Bryne?"

"He's blind," Rachel said slowly. "He can't see anything. We reran the PET scan. The area around his optic nerves is pale." She flipped on the PET's screen and displayed the last scan.

"It's probably permanent," Tolliver said matter of factly. "He'll probably be blind for the rest of his life. Does he know?"

"He knows," Rachel said. She saw the faint glow in Tolliver's eyes and stepped back as he moved to Bryne's side. Her eyes warned the others. Tolliver looked down at Bryne seeing the tears on their team leader's face and then surveyed all of them imperiously. "Babel could cure him. They had the power to regenerate life. All he has to do is accept their world, and he'll be able to see again. It should be an easy choice for Bryne. He doesn't share your primitive beliefs." Tolliver's expression made Rachel tremble. "The rest of you need to decide if you're ready to die for your faith. There's no place for your god in our world."

"We don't understand, Jim," Melea said. "What are you saying?"

"We've stumbled onto the greatest find ever made. Babel knew mass destruction was coming to their world. They froze their greatest minds in cryogenic chambers hoping they would survive. To back up that plan, they took incorporated their DNA into the genome of a skin penetrating virus. It transmitted everything about them including their knowledge into us. I don't know why you haven't been affected yet, but Carson inoculated you, Rachel. You'll be the vessel to inoculate the others. We'll be back in the morning and then your eyes should finally be open to the power."

He walked out of the laboratory area with no sign of fear on his face. He left terror in his wake.

154

CHAPTER 13

Melea recovered first. "We need to test our body secretions for the virus. If we're all still negative, we can manufacture the anti viral drugs and put them in the water supply. That may not save the others, but maybe we can slow down their assimilation. She went to the EM station and projected the virus again. "Computer, categorize unknown viral particle which will be named Virus Babel and compare it to all known viruses to prophylaxis, possible vaccine and anti viral therapy.

"Mason, pull up the data base on all known anti viral drugs and how to synthesize them." She turned back to Rachel. "I've been reading the PET database. Pale means poor blood flow. It doesn't mean dead tissue. Restart Bryne's intravenous line and give him dexamethasone 10mg and 100 micrograms of neuron growth factor. It's in the kit because of the risks of spinal cord injury."

"Have they used it in optic nerve injuries?" Rachel asked. She was grateful to have a task and reason to hope. She gathered the medical supplies and began placing the intravenous line in Bryne's arm.

"They've used it in spinal cord injuries," Melea said. "I've heard they're trying it in brain injuries. It's the best chance we can give him. The results are better in the first four hours, but we didn't know. We aren't physicians. Just give it and pray."

They had two hours to work before the sedative they had given Bryne wore off. During that time, they processed sweat and saliva samples from each of them. Virus Babel was not present in any of them. As Bryne began to strain against the restraints, Rachel had to return to her personal crisis. She had been glad for any distraction because it kept her from thinking that his refusal to fight for all their lives was admitting that he didn't really love her. She closed her hand around his restrained hand as he opened his eyes.

"Please don't fight us, Bryne. We need you to help us escape."

His fingers closed around hers only slightly. "I wanted to think it was a bad dream. I wanted to believe I'd wake up and see your face." His eyes were no longer moving as if seeking light. He was staring at the ceiling like a blind man. Rachel's voice caught in her throat as she spoke.

"Melea searched the database. Pale areas on the PET scan mean a decrease in the blood flow. It doesn't mean tissue death. We gave you steroids and neuron growth factor to help the nerves regenerate."

"They only work in the first four hours. I'm going to be blind for the rest of my life." His voice sounded matter-of-fact. "Rachel, we can't have a life like this. Even if you tell me it doesn't matter to you, I can't live with being helpless. I won't lie about how I feel or what I intend to do. You can't keep me tied up forever. When you untie me, I'm going to end my life."

She couldn't breathe because of the emotional agony his words produced. She had placed him on a pedestal and was unprepared to find he was only a man. It crumpled her resolve to be strong for him, and suddenly she knew she couldn't be strong for him. She couldn't make him want to face an uncertain future, and she couldn't keep him tied up forever.

"I gave my vow to be your wife forever. I can't make you stay with me no matter how much I love you and need you." She pulled the IV from his arm and wrapped a bandage around it. Then she unbuckled the restraints. When Bryne sat up, she put her gun in his hands. "I just want to ask you to do it now, Bryne. Do it while I'm watching so you can leave me the same legacy your mother left you. Tell me you love me and blow your brains out while I'm watching because then I'll know you told me lies so you could sleep with me. That's what Neill told me. When I watch you die, maybe I'll hate you enough to forget how much I love you." Her voice broke, and she knew he could hear she was crying.

Bryne held the gun so resolutely that Rachel had to look away. She heard him take off the safety and closed her eyes against the anticipated sound of his death. Instead she heard him sob. He put the gun down on the bed and reached out for Rachel.

"God help me," he cried. "Please help me." His words were not a echo of his mother's last words. His words were a plea for direction. Rachel couldn't understand that they were the greatest evidence he could have given to belie Neill's accusations. He was choosing to stay alive for her when he didn't want to live. Rachel put her arms around him and held him tightly.

"God will help, Bryne. I know He will, and I'm with you. You aren't alone."

He shook for a long time after his tears ceased. Rachel cried with him. When he was finally calm enough to let go of her hands, Rachel brought him food and water. She was careful to bring food he didn't have to see to consume. She put the glass in his left hand and a nutrition bar in his right hand. Both hands were shaking, but he managed to eat. Rachel found herself staring at him, wishing she could read his thoughts and then had the strange impression that it was a miracle that he could think at all. He swallowed the last bite with effort and leaned against the cot. "We have to get out of here."

"My father is making arrangements to help us." She glanced at the door uneasily. "How will we get past the others?"

"Others?" Bryne's voice was confused. "The ruins are locked down. You killed Christobal. We can just leave, can't we?"

"Something else is happening here," Melea said. "The other team members are beginning to act like Christobal. We've found a viral particle in their body fluids. It's identical to a viral particle on the ice mummies. None of us show any signs of it."

"Why don't we have it?" Bryne asked. "If it's in the environment, we should all have been infected. I touched the ice mummies. Christobal struck me before today."

"We think it could be the antiviral drugs, Bryne," Rachel said. "It's the only answer."

Bryne was silent as he tried to assimilate their hypothesis. It seemed impossible, and yet he couldn't forget how the construction workers had changed so radically. It had been easy to believe Christobal was a madman, but the workers had become violent strangers overnight.

"There's no precedent for anything like what you're suggesting," he said weakly. "It would mean they found a way for make their DNA take over cellular control. There has to be another reason."

"We can't think of any other," Melea said. She sat down beside Bryne and took his hands. "You're going to have to believe us, Bryne because we can't show you our proof. We could use your input. We don't know what else to do just now."

"I can't think," he whispered. "Get Rachel to call her father again. He can advise you." He closed his eyes to shut out the pain and the fear. He couldn't shut out his feeling of inadequacy. "If Rachel is right, God will help them." He felt immediately ashamed for even questioning his wife's faith when he was so inadequate. In that moment when he was so vulnerable, something very strange happened.

"Everything is still there," a voice said to Bryne. "You just have to believe without seeing."

"What did you say? Who was that?"

Melea was closest to him and closed her hand on his arm reassuringly. "No one, Bryne. They're working on the radio." His face looked so confused that Melea momentarily wondered what other brain damage Bryne had. Crackling from the radio interrupted her thoughts.

"I hear you, Rachel," said the colonel's voice. "I just received a transmission from Dr. Carson. He told me Dr. McAllister is infected with a strain of Cytomegalovirus. He believes you've contracted the virus from McAllister and have encephalitis. I contacted Dr. McAllister's doctor in Houston. He confirmed that McAllister has the virus. It's a sexually transmitted disease, Rachel. It can cause encephalitis and delusional behavior. Dr. Carson said you and McAllister have barricaded yourselves in the laboratory and are refusing to come out. You need to let them in. I can't help you if you don't cooperate with the rest of your team. If McAllister wants to remain in the lab, leave him."

"Bryne is my husband, Dad," she said sharply. "We're married. I know about the CMV virus. Bryne told me and gave me antiviral medicine so I wouldn't contract it. I've never been any healthier or any more frightened in my life, and the last thing I want to do is to leave the lab." She paused as she felt increasing rage at her father for being so willing to believe her enemies over her. "Did Dr. Carson explain why Melea Adams and Mason Farmer chose to lock themselves in here with us? Did you even look at the data we sent?" The radio was silent for a long moment.

"I didn't," the colonel admitted. "Everything you've told me is unbelievable, but I know you. I can't believe you're imagining this, but I can't prove you aren't until I have independent observers there. I'll dispatch a rescue mission from the base at first light, Rachel. Be ready to leave when they arrive. We'll get the four of you out of there and see what a medical examination determines."

"Thank God," she said. "We'll go whenever they can come for us, Dad, but warn them about the others. They can't afford to contact Dr. Carson or any of the others. We isolated the virus from Dr. Carson's sweat. If the virus leaves here with us..." She froze as her words made her recall her father's confinement for isolation after flights to the moon.

"You can't get us out, Dad. I should have realized it sooner." She couldn't bear to look at Mason's stricken face. "We could be responsible for the virus being transmitted to everyone on the planet. If they follow the isolation protocols ISC has, we can only be taken out of here in an isolation chamber."

The silence seemed to last a long time punctuated by the colonel's sigh.

"You're right, Rachel. If you suspect there's a risk of contagion, we can't take you out without isolation precautions."

"We'll transmit the new data we have on the virus to you," Rachel said. "Get someone at ISC to analyze it. We have two samples. One is from an ice mummy in a cryogenic chamber. The other is a swab from Dr. Carson's sweat. Our computer says they're identical. We should have gotten a sample from Christobal's blood.

They could compare his genetic material now with what it looked like before he was exposed to the virus.

"Can you get that sample?" the colonel asked. "That would be irrefutable proof."

"We can try," Rachel said. "We'll transmit the viral data now." She gave the microphone to Mason, and he began transmitting the data.

"Rachel," Melea said. "The computer just finished analyzing the virus. It contains humanoid DNA, but it's very different from our DNA." She held her breath as she looked at Bryne, praying he would resume his role as team leader. She felt he had the ability to think their way out of Babel, but he appeared to be ignoring her remark or simply unaware of its meaning.

She moved to Rachel's side to continue her report. "The base virus is similar to Ebola. The computer says it will require two drug therapy sessions to keep it from getting into the cells. The drugs it recommends are the ones we're on."

"There's nothing to be done once it's intracellular, is there?" Rachel asked.

"Nothing the computer can find. They may have to destroy the station. It may be the only way to destroy the virus. The only physical forces that can assure it's inactivated are temperatures in excess of boiling and high intensity ultraviolet light. On contact it can be killed by any number of oxidizing agents, but we can't very well flood Antarctica with liquid bleach."

"We need to give ISC a chance to analyze it," Rachel said desperately. "If they can't find an alternative, then we'll decide what will happen to us. We all know what that may mean." She surveyed the three faces and felt a surge of pity for Mason who had everything to lose. It was suddenly a blessing that she had no one who would be left alone because of her death. The thought made her sad for her father, but she wasn't afraid of that consequence like she feared what the other team members might do to them. "Let's expand the computer search to all the known virology bases while we're waiting. Maybe someone has had a theory about biological attacks with Ebola that could help us."

Bryne was lost in his own thoughts, but he was conscious of the people around him. He overheard bits and pieces of their conversations, but he didn't really absorb the feelings behind the words. He was still tempted to feel self-pity, but he kept remembering the things Rachel had said to make him put down the gun. With that memory came terrible guilt for having brought her on the dig. He had tried to believe it had been a generous offer to further her career, but it seemed likely she was risking her life with very little chance of return. She was married to a blind man and trapped in a site from which they might not ever recover anything of value. He spent some time thinking of how he could improve the return on her investment and had to admit that any outcome was out of his hands. Ultimately he wanted to apologize to her and know she could forgive him. Several hours later while the others were still scanning computer files, he called out to Rachel. He could feel the tension in her hand as she touched his arm.

"I'm sorry I brought you here," he said. "I never thought you'd be threatened. I swear I didn't bring you here for the reason Neill said. I wanted a permanent relationship with you. When I made the wager with Neill, it was about getting you to be interested in the same way. I never said anything about seduction. I want you to believe that, and I don't think you do anymore."

"I don't know what I believe right now," she said and knew it was true. She felt an unreasonable anger against him because of her father's suffering. "I'm focused on getting us out of here. There may not be any way to make that happen, but I guess that outcome would be good for you. You won't have to worry about living as a blind man."

His face showed shock and then slow realization. Rachel had to realize that he wasn't absorbing the crux of their situation. She felt guilty for depriving him of the bliss of ignorance. "Don't worry about it, Bryne. There's nothing you can do, and I don't blame you. I chose to come here, and I'm responsible for my own destiny." She started to move away, but he grasped her arm desperately. "I won't let you die here, Rachel. I won't."

"I don't think any of us has much control over that variable just now." She started to move away, but he sat up and kept his hold on her arm. Suddenly he was overcome with the need to do something. "Can you take me to the computer station?"

"What are you going to do?" she asked.

"I need to hear a summary of everything that's happening. I thought I could listen while you keep working."

She gave in to his request thinking it was probably a waste of his time, but then it would pass whatever time they might have left. The radio had remained ominously silent, which meant to Rachel that her father was also exhausting all the options. Bryne leaned heavily on her due to his knee injury and sank into the chair in front of the terminal. He gave the voice commands establishing his identity and put on a headset as if he could see it. He could feel Rachel walking away as he asked the computer to summarize all station logs since his injury. Then he began a tortured effort to understand what the words meant. Helpless frustration welled inside him as he heard enough to know they were probably destined to die. It would be the only choice for the military when they realized the potential of the Babel virus. He thought he should be able to think of another way to destroy the virus, but his mind was moving like an outdated computer with limited memory. The prayer to get Rachel out of danger seemed to arise from the depths of his soul to a God who was still a stranger to him. "I probably deserve to die, but these others don't. They follow You. If you can help me think them out of this place, I'll believe without any more questions and You can do whatever You want to do with me."

In the midst of the sounds of the machinery, he remembered his work in the military on bioterrorism defense systems. "We'll have to kill the others to destroy the mobile sources of the virus," he said tentatively. "We could detonate ultraviolet bombs through the facility if we can prove the virus is killed with ultraviolet radiation. Do we still have an ice mummy here?"

"Yes," Melea said hopefully. "It's heavily infected with the virus."

"Computer, can the morgue containers be sealed off from the rest of the laboratory?" Bryne asked.

"Yes," said the computer.

"Computer, pull up bioterrorism file 179843 from the UKM5 office. Authorization BJMA467."

"Accessing," the computer said.

"When the file opens, there should be instructions on building several different types of ultraviolet bombs," Bryne said. "Copy all of them to the station computer under my security codes. Then synthesize the materials we'll need to build the bomb labeled single source decontamination." He paused and then added, "Isolate all laboratory computer activity from any other terminal on the station and give access only to the four team members present in this room."

"Terminal lock down implemented," the computer replied. "M5 files copied. Supplies for single source contamination are available in the laboratory storage unit."

"Check availability for building large area sterilization and a laminar flow ultraviolet chamber. Identify maximal levels of ultraviolet radiation tolerable to human life but lethal to virus Babel with hypothesis to be confirmed after single source contamination test."

He felt Rachel lean over his shoulder and let the scent of her body confirm it was her as he reached for her hand. "I need you and Melea to go over the single source instructions step by step. I can explain how to carry out anything you question."

"What are you going to do?" Rachel and Melea asked at the same time.

"The single source bomb will test if we can kill the virus with ultraviolet light. If we can, we'll build the bigger unit to kill the other team members and the viral particles in the ruins. Then we can build a laminar flow ultraviolet chamber to sterilize anything on our skin as we exit and set off another bomb to sterilize the upper chamber at a later date."

There was a moment of silence as the other team members realized the plan might work and then a flurry of activity. Rachel squeezed his shoulder. "I'll let Dad know and then start gathering your materials."

He caught her arm with the desperate grip of an embarrassed stranger. "Before you go, could you help me get to the loo?"

He was glad she just helped him up without making a verbal response. Then he was glad for the pain in his knee because it kept him from making an emotional response to the most tangible sign of his dependence. He ran into the urinal and almost fell, but he repelled Rachel's steadying hand.

"If you'd wait outside, it will be easier for me," he said in a strained voice.

"Bryne," she began.

"Please," he said. "Please."

He had the feeling he might be voiding on his shoes and fought the urge to cry. He stood at the sink for so long that Rachel looked into the bathroom to make sure he was all right. He pressed his hands to his face as if washing it.

"I'm ready," he said. "Your father will probably have questions, but I don't want the other team members to know my source. They might find some way to stop us."

"Are you all right?" she asked tentatively.

"I'll get you out of here," he said. "I've prayed to get you out of here. That's keeping me in focus."

He looked beaten, and she wanted to comfort him. Something told her it wouldn't be possible before she embraced him. He pressed one hand against her back. "Let's go. We may not have much time to get this done."

The radio reached ISC without difficulty that time. A breathless colonel answered the summons. "What's happening, Rachel?"

"Have you analyzed the data, Dad?"

"We have," he said somberly. "The virologist here says the virus is carrying a complete human genome. It's skin penetrating. It won't be easy to eradicate. I have everyone working on it."

"You believe me?" she asked with relief.

"Carson called us directly," the colonel said. "They modified the radio to cut through the storm. When I asked him about the virus, he laughed and said he'd explain it in person. Rachel, I don't know what we'll be able to do. If we follow the bioterrorism protocol..."

"Bryne has an idea," Rachel interrupted. "I can't tell you all of it because we're afraid they might have access to this transmission. Can you give us some time?"

"I've put the station on satellite monitoring," the colonel said. "If I see any signs of anyone leaving, I'll have to act. I thought McAllister was disabled."

"He's injured, but he's come up with a plan. He worked with a bioterrorism unit when he was in military service."

"I'll be praying he's right," the colonel said tersely. "Keep me informed."

As Rachel closed the connection, Melea and Mason closed ranks around her. Bryne didn't give any of them time to discuss the option of failure. He began assigning tasks to build the test device. It took them two hours.

CHAPTER 14

They sealed the single source device inside the morgue vault with the ice mummy. The computer confirmed the vault was sealed before Bryne detonated the device. The room vibrated faintly, but the force of the explosion was much less than Rachel expected. At Bryne's direction they gave the vault thirty minutes of air flow to cool it. When the vault was opened, there was no need to swab the body. Only ashes remained on the table. Melea was shaking as she took a sample and made slides for the electron microscope. No viral particles could be found.

"I think we can say the test was a success," Bryne said grimly. "Now we need to build the larger model."

"What will you use to mix the components?" Melea asked.

"The extra reactor core," Bryne said. We'll need to decide the safest place for us to be when we detonate it."

"The generator room," Melea said. "It's radiation safe so we should be safe there."

"Computer, audio interface. Command code BJMA68."

"Audio interface on line," the computer said.

"Identify any radiation safe areas within the Babel ruins," Bryne said.

"Three intact cryogenic chambers exist within the ruins. These are radiation safe." The computer's voice was matter of fact.

"We need to disable their doors," Bryne said. "An old fashioned kitchen sink bomb should manage that task nicely."

Bryne had to take pain pills to stay with them through the night. Aside from the pain, his head injury had produced a profound disturbance in his balance. He would have fallen more than once, but Rachel stayed beside him to steady him. Despite the drugs and his injuries, his thoughts became progressively clearer. Bryne knew that defied the standard progression of an injury like his, and he began to believe that his prayer was being answered.

When the bombs were complete, they hid them in the sterilized morgue compartment though they didn't intend to voluntarily admit the other team members again. Melea and Mason stretched out to sleep for three hours. Rachel took guard duty expecting to be alone. Bryne remained with her.

"How much ammunition do you have left?" he asked.

"More than half this clip and another one." Rachel looked at her husband and felt pity. It wasn't difficult to see he was still in pain despite the medication he had taken. "Lie down, Bryne. You can put your head in my lap."

"That might be too good an offer to refuse," Bryne said. He eased himself down, grimacing from the pain of his broken ribs. Rachel's lap supported his head so that his neck stopped throbbing for the first time in hours. Her hands were soothing as they stroked his forehead and hair. He tried to ignore the impression that she was only being kind.

"I'm all right, Rachel. I can handle this." He flushed as he realized he sounded as uncertain as he felt.

"No one expects you to be superhuman," she said. He could feel her sigh. "We're all afraid for very personal reasons."

"I was afraid, but now I just feel numb." His eyes stared at the ceiling as if he could count every defect in the tiles. He couldn't see anything but pervasive darkness. "If this were some sort of punishment for me, you and the others certainly didn't earn it. I used to do things I knew were morally wrong and then shake my fist at God. I thought the fact that He didn't strike me dead was proof He didn't exist. At first, it was a rush. It was proof there wasn't a God. Now I really hope you and Melea are right. I hope there's a God and He'll get you safely away. He can be assured I'll give Him all the credit. I'm helpless to do anything except think and remember." He paused. "It's odd how I never thought about my family's deaths as cowardice. My mother didn't have your faith or Melea's. My sisters died because she was a coward. So is her son. Perhaps your courage is the greatest proof of God's existence."

"I'm not in control of my life, Bryne. I've never believed I was. I've always believed there was a purpose in everything that happens to me. Even if we don't live to get away from here, maybe letting the world know what was in the Babel records will change some people. I've transmitted everything we've found to my father and the ISC. I hope you'll understand and not be angry."

"I could never be angry with you, Rachel. You are the sort of person everyone should be. I feel very small in your presence." He felt tears on his face and pressed his hands against his eyes. "I'm sorry. I haven't shed a tear in years and now I can't stop crying. Yet another sign that I'm not in control of anything anymore, if I ever really was. If God wants me on my knees, He has achieved His goal."

"I don't think God wants people beaten into submission, Bryne. He just wants them looking up. Maybe everything around you was too distracting. You don't know what God will let happen. I believe in miracles." Fleetingly she thought of Dr. Carson and then Tolliver's last visit. Her hand was tense and communicated the worry to Bryne.

"What are you thinking?" Bryne asked.

"I was thinking about Tolliver. He's been infected by the virus. I guess he was infected when he used the laser to stop the bleeding in your head."

"What?" Bryne looked confused. "What did he do?"

"You were bleeding in the back of your brain. In your brain stem. We could see the clot forming. We gave you platelet aggregation factor, and then Tolliver used the laser to drain the clot and to seal off the bleeding vessel."

"He couldn't do that, Rachel," Bryne said slowly. "I've taken every emergency course offered to lay people. He could use the laser to make a burr hole, but if he did anything that went through brain tissue he'd be destroying nerve cells. If he was already becoming a part of Babel, he probably cut my optic nerves deliberately because he knew I'd be less of a threat if I were blind."

Rachel felt sick with guilt, and she struggled to rationalize what had happened. "You would have died, Bryne. I didn't know he was infected. None of the rest of us knew what to do."

"It's not your fault," he said. "You couldn't have known, and I would have died." He sat up slowly. "In a strange way it makes me feel better to know God didn't do it to punish me."

"Tolliver came here after we knew you were blind," Rachel said. "He said Babel could give you back your sight if you followed them. He's coming back in the morning."

"It isn't worth their price," Bryne said fiercely. "They're asking for my immortal soul. I always thought that was what worshipping God was about. Of the two choices, I think I'll stay with your faith and my blindness." He lay back slowly and thought of the impossibility of escape. "I need to think," he said. "I need to think of how we can get out of here." He closed his eyes and felt himself praying again for the others. The heavy pain in his head eased with the repeated thought, and he dozed while Rachel stroked his hair and prayed. Sometime during their watch, the plan began to take shape in Bryne's mind.

CHAPTER 15

The radio summoned them at five in the morning. Mason awakened Rachel. She was able to slip a pillow under Bryne's head and slip away without awakening him.

"The infectious disease specialists say this has the potential to be a plague," the colonel said. "Simulations show the virus inserting itself into the nuclei of cells and deleting the active genome. The genetic material is dissimilar to every known population on the planet."

"Bryne has a plan that might let us destroy the virus, Dad. If it works, we might even live to tell the tale. Did you talk to Dr. Carson again?"

"Last night," the colonel said. "He still insists that you and Bryne are insane. Rachel, you understand what will happen if you fail? I don't have any choice."

"I know, Dad. It's all right. If we don't succeed, you need to destroy the station. Melea ran simulations. The virus can be destroyed by UV radiation, oxidizing agents or extreme heat."

"If we have to do it, we'll use something that will extinguish all life instantly." His voice broke. "If McAllister's idea works, radio me. We'll get you out between storms. How long will it take?"

"Give us seventy-two hours," she said. "I love you, Daddy. Erebus station out."

She pulled Melea and Mason to the far side of the lab. "The extra containment unit is in storage compartment one. I think Bryne put the damaged one there, too. We need to get them."

"We need the probe, too," Bryne's voice said. He was walking toward them along the periphery of the room. His left hand was keeping his position. He was limping slightly from the injury to his knee, but his expression kept Rachel from going to him until he reached the open chemistry bench. She took his arm when he hesitated because he could feel the bench in front of his leg.

"Why do we need the probe?" she asked as he moved with her.

"We can use it to deliver the bombs into the cryogenic chambers. There's no other way to get them down there. I'm the only one who has been there, and there are too many places we could be trapped. We could send the probe down tonight. They'll have to sleep at some point."

"It's a good idea," Mason said. "I'll go with Rachel to get the equipment."

"We probably should wait for Tolliver to come back," Rachel said. "If he sees us gone, he'll alert the others."

"Maybe we should just kill him," Melea said. "He's not our colleague now."

"If we kill him, we may bring them down on us," Bryne said. "We need to make them believe we've summoned help from the base through Rachel's father. Then they'll be thinking about how to dominate that situation and give us time to dominate them." His eyes didn't seek Rachel out, but she knew his next words were for her. "If you encounter them on the way to the storerooms, kill them. There are seven of them. I'd like to see us even up the odds."

They were eating when Tolliver returned. Rachel made Bryne's food and put it in his hands before sitting down with her own meal. When she sat down, Bryne turned his face toward her.

"I can see some light," he said. "Nothing beyond that, but it's something." Tolliver knocked before she could respond. Rachel moved to Bryne's other side, and she took the safety off the gun. Melea opened the door. Tolliver was alone, and he entered with his eyes on Bryne. He seemed pleased when Bryne's eyes didn't focus on him.

"I'm terribly sorry about your vision, McAllister," Tolliver said. "It's a tremendous blow, isn't it?"

"Nothing I can't manage," Bryne said tersely. "All proprieties aside, what do you want from us?"

"We want you," Tolliver said. "Not really you, but your brain. We lost several of our greatest minds when the cryogenic chambers failed. We inoculated the construction workers, but there's no great intellect being produced. We want your brain, and in exchange you'll be able to see again."

"Give up who I am and my soul to have my sight back," Bryne said. "I don't know. That just doesn't seem to be an even exchange, Tolliver. I guess I'll have to stay here and learn to be blind."

Tolliver's hand struck Bryne quickly and with superhuman strength. As he plunged towards Bryne, Rachel pulled out the gun and shot Tolliver. The scientist looked shocked as he fell dead. Melea pressed the button to close the door but not before one of the construction workers ran into the room. Rachel also fired at him, but her aim served only to wound that enemy. He flung himself into Rachel, and they fell to the floor wrestling for the gun. Mason slammed a pipe left over from their bomb making into the worker's head crushing his skull.

"Rachel!" Bryne shouted frantically. "Where's Rachel?"

"I'm here on the floor," she said. She couldn't get up until Mason dragged the body off her. By then, Bryne had crawled to her side.

"Are you all right?" he asked.

"I'm fine," she panted. "And our odds are better. Six to four in their favor." She touched the wound on his face. "Are you all right?"

"I'm ready to fight." He stood unsteadily and helped Rachel up. They held onto each other as they returned to the table. When they could regroup, they took blood samples from Tolliver's body, extracted samples of his DNA from the white cell nuclei and transmitted the genetic map of who Tolliver had become to Colonel Madison. They put both bodies in the freezer with the ice mummies.

Bryne was momentarily glad he couldn't see when Mason and Rachel left the lab to obtain the supplies they needed. The feeling rapidly subsided, leaving him overwhelmed by helplessness. Melea sat down beside him and took his hand.

"I have the other gun, but we only have a half clip of ammunition," she told him.

"If Rachel and Mason don't make it back, it won't matter," he said. He faced the sound of her voice and held the memory of her face. He could almost feel her gently sympathetic smile. "You aren't afraid of what our outcome will be."

"I'll be with my family again if we don't make it, and I'll be able to watch you and Rachel have your life together if we do. I don't dwell on what I can't change, Bryne. That's the only way I survived what happened in Egypt."

"It was my fault," he said. "I suppose you've always known that, but I wanted you to know I knew it was my fault. Arielle and I had a row about my lack of faith and the lies I had told her to get her to accept my proposal. I accused her of going along with the lies because she needed me even more than I needed her." He looked away from Melea as if he could meet her gaze and feel more anguish. "She went on with the dig without me to prove she didn't need me in any way. I have wanted to beg her forgiveness for a long time."

"If you want her forgiveness, Bryne, don't lie to Rachel. Arielle wanted you to have faith. I think she would have been willing to die to give you that comfort, but we talked that night. She told me everything, and we knew she was going to have to be patient. Then she had this idea that what we found under the sphinx would help you see the meaning of faith. Her father agreed. We were all very content that night. You can't know when your time has come, but I know it was their time. It had nothing to do with you. They would have gone anyway. What you need to ask yourself is what I've asked myself a million times. Why are we still here? I know there's a reason. Maybe we were meant to share this with the world as a warning."

"I couldn't ask for that," Bryne said grimly. "I'm just praying to get the three of you out of here. I'm not really in any position to make a deal with God, but I told Him I'd accept whatever happens to me without questions if he spares the three of you."

Melea was surprised and glad that Bryne couldn't see her face. She was very certain at that moment that Bryne had prayed for them and in a selfless way. She thought of her daughter and then put her arms around the man Arielle had loved. The silence felt comforting to them both. "I suppose I will have to do the same for you," she said quietly. "I can't imagine life without you."

Rachel and Mason moved without speaking. They slipped along the walls covering each other until they reached the westernmost part of the dome and the storage chambers. They found the two containment cores easily. The probe required much more time. It wasn't in the first or second storage room. They found it under a tarp in the third room. Rachel had to pocket the gun to help Mason free it. She held her breath until they were ready to leave and then realized she would have to carry some of the load.

"Wait," Mason whispered as he rigged a backpack-like sling to carry the probe. Rachel was helping him shoulder the load when she realized the door was swinging slowly shut. They threw themselves against it slamming Armand to the ground. Rachel shoved the gun into his face.

"Get up and walk in front of me," she ordered the Frenchman.

"And you will make me do this?" he said arrogantly. He kicked Rachel's legs knocking her against the door. Before she recovered enough to pull the trigger, he was almost on her. She fired three times before he fell. Mason helped her scramble to her feet and they ran back to the laboratory, not caring how much noise they made. Melea opened the door to admit them, and they slid into the room like runners sliding into a base. Melea closed the door as they all heard the sounds of the pursuit.

"We got the equipment," Rachel gasped. "We also got Armand."

"We have better odds then," Bryne said as he reached out for her. He held Rachel in his arms for a long moment. "Mason, I need to teach you how to use the probe."

They rested in shifts, which was no easy task. The greatest distraction to their effort was the sound of their enemies moving in the corridor outside the laboratory door. Bryne never really slept at all as he mulled over every facet of his plan to sterilize the base. He spent the afternoon making Mason familiar with the probe's controls. As night drew near, he gave Mason and Melea instructions on how to modify the probe's robotic arm to lift the pipe bombs from its cargo area.

"Play back your recordings of the ruins," Bryne told Mason. "Program the route I took to get to the lower level into the probe's remote. The last three doors on the right were intact. The probe needs to push one of the pipes into the ice at the base of each door." He stood and moved toward the laboratory bench where the containment cores were sitting. He was able to cross the distance safely by holding his hands in front of him and sliding his feet forward. His hands found the cores as Rachel watched. She knew she shouldn't offer him any help until he asked for it.

"Rachel," he said. "I need you to plug my computer interface into this core."

When he heard the cable snap into place, he put his hands on the keyboard almost tentatively. "Are my hands positioned?"

"They are," Rachel said.

He typed in a sign on code and then a command.

"Audio interface," the computer said.

"Computer, measure current fuel contents of the containment core."

The computer's voice and screen reeled off a list of components consisting primarily of hydrogen and helium. "Computer, print one copy." Bryne's hand found Rachel's arm. "Make a clipboard of the printed sheets, Rachel. I need to keep a running tally of what's in there and what we've added."

"A nuclear recipe," she said to lighten the moment.

"One that can't afford any variance by the cooks," he said grimly. "Computer, access the file, solar sterilization. Print one copy of this file." He waited until the printer was silent and then said, "Calculate the chemical additives necessary to carry out solar flare 2 experiment using the attached containment core. Print the additive list."

"Sodium, iron, nitrogen, oxygen, sulfur," Rachel read. "Don't you have to have pressure and heat to start the fusion reaction?"

"Solar flare 2 is a duplication of the reactions on the surface of the sun. All we need is 5700° Kelvin to get the right temperature. This core can get the pressure head of an autoclave on full cycle after you deliver the heat. We'll ignite phosphorus to do that."

He took the sheet as it emerged from the printer. "Put this into the chemistry station scanner and ask the station computer to come up on 9214 Lynx. Then ask it to fill a nuclear safe syringe with these components. Those are the titanium ones in the drawer."

As she hurried to do his bidding, he ordered the computer to configure a triggering charge of phosphorus. "Mason, make me a remote control device that will trigger an electrical charge on the outside of the containment unit. Computer, analyze the scatter pattern of the ultraviolet radiation potentially produced by the detonation of solar flare 2 in the Babel ruins. Is the scatter pattern sufficient to sterilize all life forms within this dome?"

"Scatter pattern is sufficient to eradicate all life including viral life within a one mile radius," the computer replied.

"Will the eradication include virus Babel?" Bryne asked.

"Virus Babel has a 99.99% chance of deactivation if exposed to solar flare 2," the computer reassured him. "Viral particles in radiation safe areas would have a 84.6% chance of survival."

"Computer, scan station generator room for any evidence of Virus Babel?"

"Such a scan would require four hours," the computer said.

Bryne was hesitating to give the command when he heard a faint sound above them. The meaning of the sound was slow to penetrate his mind. When it did, he sprang to address it.

"Get away from the walls! Are you all clear?" He heard the three voices say clear. "Computer, electrify the laboratory walls and ceiling of the laboratory."

They all heard the scream and smelled the sickening odor of burning flesh.

"End electrical charge," Bryne said. He tried not to think of what he had done. It took him a moment to overcome the feeling. "Someone was coming to us via the ceiling crawl space. I hadn't thought of that as being a threat. Computer generate warning alarm and repeat charge if any movement is detected above or below this room. Lock out all other users on main frame except McAllister, Adams, Farmer and Madison. Use voice print analysis to confirm identification. Lock down generator room. Access only to voice command. Authorization BJMA68."

"Main frame locked. Generator room cannot be sealed due to presence of a human life form inside the room."

"That's bad," Bryne said under his breath. "Computer, can you identify the person in the generator room?"

"Person in the generator room is Carson, Neill," the computer replied.

"Computer, lock out generator control functions." Bryne's voice betrayed his anxiety.

"Generator control functions have already been locked out by Carson, Neill." The voice was maddeningly impassive.

"Computer, what is the status of the current intradome temperature?" As Bryne asked the question, all three of the people confined with him realized what was happening.

"The current intradome temperature is 68°F and falling at a rate of 10 degrees per hour."

"He's turned off the generator," Melea breathed.

"He's turned down the thermostat," Bryne said slowly. "They have some way to tolerate the cold that we don't have. They probably want us to try and go into the generator room so they can corner us." He put his hand on the laboratory bench for balance. "Mason, see if you can isolate a root command to give us control over the thermostat functions. If you can get around whatever Carson did, I won't let him get a second shot at it."

He moved around the wall slowly and sat down on the cot at the far end of the room. Rachel followed him and put her arms around him.

"We'll just pray harder, Bryne," she said slowly. "Mason will find a way."

"We've got to get the cryogenic chambers disabled tonight. Then we need to set off the bomb. That's assuming we can get the thermostatic controls under our control." He put his hand on her face almost as if he could see it. The movement to get there might have been construed as a caress instead of the searching hand of a blind man. As he touched her, Bryne felt as if he could see Rachel's face and lost himself in the feeling it had engendered the first time he had seen her.

"I love you, Rachel," he said. "You might not ever know how much. I'm glad your face was the last thing I saw."

His hand felt different, and at that moment, she forgot to feel pity or anything but love. His words made her afraid. "You sound like you're saying goodbye."

"No, I'm not. I just need to know you believe me and can forgive me. If this doesn't turn out as we hope, I don't want that on my conscience as well. I had no right to complain when everyone else might give up so much more. I've been a very arrogant man for a long time. I didn't think of myself that way. I felt I was very humanitarian, but now I can see very clearly what was before my eyes for years. Can you forgive me?"

She knew he had lied to her about believing, but in the same way, she knew he was now telling her the truth. She held his hands against her face and nodded. "We're meant to be together. I'll always believe that God moves in mysterious ways." Mason's victorious cry interrupted them.

"Success!" he said. "I've isolated the thermostat function. What now?"

Bryne let Rachel lead him back to the computer. "Computer, audio interface."

"Recognize McAllister," the computer said.

"Return all thermostat functions to central computer control."

"Thermostat functions are being manually held," the computer said.

"Computer, disable the manual thermostat controls." Bryne's voice sounded tentative for the first time.

"Manual thermostat controls disabled," the computer said.

"Lock the thermostat at the current ambient temperature." He pressed his hand against Rachel's cross as he gave the command. The pause for the computer to answer seemed interminable.

"Thermostat locked at 48°F."

"Thank God," said the collective sigh.

"Close general dome controls. Save all changes." Bryne exhaled and reached toward Rachel until she took his hand. "We can't afford to give them any time to counteract that. I need to load the containment core now. Melea, will you help me? Mason has children, and Rachel could be pregnant."

"I'll help you," Melea said without hesitation." She went to retrieve the titanium syringe.

179

It was just after midnight when Bryne injected the trace elements into the core and attached the phosphorus trigger. "OK," he said. "We can only do a field test." He put his hands on the keyboard and typed in his sign on code and the command for audio interface. "Computer, locate all the living occupants of the dome including any possible humanoid intruders."

"Adams, Farmer, Madison and McAllister are located in the central laboratory. Carson is in his quarters. Gibar is in his quarters. Landers is in his quarters. Davidson is at the drill shaft."

"Current sleep cycle status of Davidson?" Bryne asked.

"Davidson fits the parameters for being awake," the computer said.

"We've got to take him out quietly," Bryne said. "How are we supplied with tranquilizers, Melea?"

"We have enough to put all of them out," she said. "What do you want?"

"An air syringe with enough ketamine to knock out an elephant. We don't care about potential euthanasia today. We just need to make sure we get enough to neutralize him."

CHAPTER 16

They packed to leave the laboratory as a group, knowing if they were successful they would go to the generator room to take refuge. For that reason they took all their food and the rest of their water supply. As they were leaving, Bryne used his voice command to seal the laboratory area.

Their plan was very simple. When they reached the area outside the drill site, Bryne entered the area leaving the others to watch. He moved around the periphery of the room carrying the probe. As the others watched, Davidson left his guard post and began stalking Bryne. When he was near the door, Rachel stepped out and pointed the gun at Davidson.

"I've shot all the others. It didn't bother me a bit. Lie face down on the floor."

Davidson's eyes glowed as he looked at Rachel, but her hands were braced with her finger curled around the trigger. The posture convinced him to lay down on the floor. The minute he was down, Mason put a knee in Davidson's back to hold him. Melea administered the injection, and they held him until he was unconscious.

"He's out of commission, Bryne," Rachel whispered. She led him to the drill site, and he unwound the tether around the probe. They lowered it carefully until it was in the ruins and then released the tether.

"Let's go," Bryne whispered.

They moved silently through the corridors and back into the laboratory. Mason hurried to start the probe along its preprogrammed path. They didn't illuminate its path. They simply watched the tracking path on the computer screen and prayed.

The twenty-minute journey seemed to take an eternity. When the tracking path said they were in the lowest level, Mason illuminated the area. The probe delivered the bomb and then withdrew to the next level.

"Put it behind the bodies on the second level," Bryne said. "Then the others won't see it when they come to see what happened." Mason complied, using the light to assure them of the probe's position.

"We're parked, Bryne."

"Detonate," Bryne said.

The explosion shook the entire dome and told them they had been successful without any need for them to see the results. All of them patted Bryne on the back.

"Computer," Bryne said. "Are any of the cryogenic chambers radiation-safe at this time?"

"There are no radiation-safe cryogenic chambers," the computer replied.

"That's just step one," Bryne said. "The big hurdle is step two. They'll be searching the station. Let's get some rest and take shifts standing guard."

They ate, and Mason and Melea took the first shift to sleep. Bryne signed onto the computer and opened the audio interface.

"Computer, give locations of all humanoid life forms in Erebus station and ruins," he said.

"Adams, Farmer, Madison and McAllister are in the laboratory area. Carson and Gibar are in the ruins. Landers is at the drill site," the computer said.

"Location of Davidson?" Bryne asked.

"Life form Davidson had vital sign cessation at 0100 hours," the computer replied.

"Well, that's three to four odds," Bryne said.

"Don't we need to inject the other containment core now?" Rachel asked.

"There's a crack in it," Bryne said. "I can't see it, but it's big enough for me to feel. If we try to inject it with the admixture, the pressure might cause it to explode."

182

"Can we get everything in the station sterilized with just the one?" Rachel asked.

"Maybe not," Bryne conceded. "That one has to be detonated on the lower level in the ruins to get as much as we can. If we can eliminate the others, then we can seal the shaft and gradually sterilize the upper level. We'll be safe from virus Babel as long as the drugs last. The problem will be in getting all of them into the ruins." The nagging idea in the back of his mind jumped forward as if to tell him it was the only solution. He accepted it as the answer to his prayer because he wanted Rachel to live more than he had ever wanted anything. He was silent so long that Rachel prodded him.

"How can we sterilize the upper level?"

"We can get your father to air drop oxidizing solution and UV light units to sterilize the upper levels if there's still identifiable virus. We'll have to sterilize ourselves, too. We'll have it on our skin even if the drugs keep protecting us."

"That might take a long time," Rachel said.

"That could take the rest of the Antarctic winter, but the station is equipped to last until then. Rachel, we've got to do this no matter what the price. You know that."

"I know," she said. "My dad fully intends to wipe out the station if we aren't successful." She looked at him and suddenly realized where the conversation was going. "What are you saying?"

"I need to take the bomb down to them. If I go down into the ruins, they'll follow me, and we'll be guaranteed to have them together when the bomb is detonated. I can make them think I've decided to get my sight back at any price. I'm the one they want, and really I'm the one who should go. Mason has children. I couldn't let you or Melea go. I'd need you to take care of Melea for me. In an odd sort of way she's been my mother and I've been her son."

"No," Rachel said. She knew he wasn't suggesting suicide. She knew he was intending to martyr himself. "Please think of any other way. Please, Bryne. It's going to work no matter how we get it down there. We can track down the others. We can kill them and then sterilize the ruins."

"We've been lucky so far. If we make one mistake, any or all of us could die instead of them. We aren't the only ones at risk. If they escape from Erebus, they could destroy our world. I want you to live, and I'm willing to die to make sure that happens. At least I can do this to keep you safe. I remember reading something in the Bible like that. It said husbands should love their wives like Christ loved the church. I do love you that much. It's the first time I've ever felt that way."

"How do you remember so much from a book you said you didn't believe?" She held onto him with both hands. "I love you so much. Please think of any other way. Please, Bryne. Promise me you'll try."

"I promise," he said quietly. "We'll try."

"Maybe I'm pregnant," Rachel said desperately. "Maybe you're going to be a father. You can't leave us." She knew she would have faced anything, even her own death, with greater courage than what he was suggesting called for. "Please don't leave me."

"Don't think about it now," he said quietly. He pulled her head down on his shoulder and stroked her hair until he could feel she wasn't crying. Then he sat down, leaning against the lab bench and holding her against him. He continued to caress her hair until she was asleep in his arms.

"Computer, set up a surveillance alarm if anyone enters the corridor outside of laboratory." He turned his head in response to the noise of Mason's approach.

"Surveillance alarm set," the computer said.

"Mason?" Bryne said.

"I'm here," Mason replied. "I thought you might need to sleep."

"Actually I wanted to talk to you," Bryne said. "I wish I could put Rachel down. Could you spread some blankets?"

"Sure," Mason said. His footsteps told Bryne he was returned to the other side of the room and was bringing back the covers he had used. He spread them beside Bryne, and Bryne eased Rachel down, leaving her head resting on his leg. She stirred once and then slept uninterrupted like a exhausted child. Mason sat down beside Bryne who pulled the laptop computer terminal into his lap.

"Tell me if my hands are right," Bryne asked.

"They're right." Mason read the screen as Bryne began typing his will.

I, Bryne Jacob McAllister, being of sound mind do hereby revoke any previous wills I have made in order for this document to take precedence over them. Rachel Leah Madison is my wife and sole heir having married me on the Antarctica continent under international law in a ceremony performed by Mason Farmer, a duly licensed minister. I hereby bequeath all my possessions to Rachel Madison McAllister to include any salaries, stipends or royalties owed me at the time of my death. Given this day in June, 2010 by my hand.
Signed,
Bryne Jacob McAllister, Ph.D.

Bryne typed in the command to print the document. "I need you to make sure I'm signing in the right place."

"Why are you doing this, Bryne?" Mason asked. "Do you think we aren't going to make it out of here?"

"You'll make it out. Do you have a pen?"

Mason put the paper on the floor and put a pen in Bryne's hand with his hand over it. Bryne signed the paper as if he could see it.

"Witness it for me, Mason, and make another copy." Bryne put his hand on Rachel's hair. "Computer, give the location of Carson, Gibar and Landers."

"Carson and Gibar are in the ruins. Landers is at the drill shaft," the computer replied.

Mason put the documents into Bryne's hand. "When will we set off the bomb?"

"I need you to keep these for Rachel," Bryne said. "I also need to give you a list of everything to do afterwards. Do you have something to write on or do you want to use the computer?"

"Please answer me," Mason demanded. "What are you planning to do?"

"Get us out in any way I can," Bryne said. "Could you change from your minister's hat for a minute?"

Mason sat down slowly. "Suicide is wrong, Bryne."

"That's not what this is about, Mason. We've got to stop these people. We have to stop them. If we don't, we'll be allowing a plague loose on the world. Suicide and martyrdom are not synonymous. Please make the list."

"I'm ready," Mason said grudgingly.

"Get Rachel to radio her father. You'll need UV lights to sterilize all the upper levels and oxidizing agent safe to sterilize human skin. You'll have to stay on the anti viral drugs for at least a couple of months. Make sure they air drop enough for all of you. Lock down the drill shaft and just analyze the data. All of you have access to the command functions, and there will be enough food and water until winter's end. Don't go down into the ruins. The next team can recover what's left of us."

"Tell me why we can't just hunt down the other three?" Mason asked.

"We're running out of time. They'll find a way to trap us and kill us. There aren't that many bullets left. I told Rachel, but please help her understand this is the only way." He paused. "I don't want to die, you know. I did when I knew I was blind, but now I don't. I think I could live feeling like there is something so much greater than myself watching over me. I never felt that until now." His voice broke. "I haven't lived the way all of you have. Do you think I still have any chance — of heaven?"

Mason gripped his hand. "I know you do. It isn't what we were that makes the difference, Bryne. It's what God molds us into."

The lights dimmed suddenly, and Mason's sharp intake of breath made Bryne aware of the change even before the darkness around him deepened. "The lights are out."

"They're coming," Bryne said simply.

"Proximity alarm," the computer said. "Carson and Gibar are in the outer corridor."

Bryne spoke Melea's name almost soundlessly, and Mason hurried to awaken her. His hand shaking Rachel's shoulder awakened her. They gathered beside the computer for light. Only Bryne didn't need the light. Strangely, he felt as if a lighted map of the station were inside his mind.

"Get up in the crawl space and crawl 25 yards straight north," Bryne whispered. "You'll cross eight and a half of the ceiling tiles. That will be dead center over the generator room. They must have cut the wires to this quarter of the dome. They don't dare cut the power to the generator. When you get there, put in the command for perimeter alarm and electrify the area if anyone sets off the alarm. Give me the core and the remote."

Mason returned with the core and remote. He stuffed the containment core into the bottom of a rappelling backpack. Bryne took them as if he could see while putting a pocket compass into Mason's hands. He gave the lap top to Rachel. Melea had already climbed up on the counter top and pushed aside the ceiling tile. Bryne was putting on the backpack while the others climbed up. He put the detonator into his right pants pocket.

Melea entered the crawl space first followed by Rachel. Both of them stifled a gasp as they crawled past the charred body of one of the workers. Neither of the two women knew Bryne wasn't following until they reached the generator room. Mason knew when Bryne was no longer touching him as a guide, but he thought the team leader was following by listening.

"Where's Bryne?" Rachel asked hysterically. Mason looked back into the crawl space and couldn't answer her. He restrained Rachel from climbing back up with difficulty.

"Let him do it, Rachel," Mason pleaded. "Bryne prayed to know what to do. He's probably our only chance." When she gave up the struggle, she collapsed on the floor sobbing and begging God to spare her husband.

Bryne had memorized every square foot of the station plans long before its completion and he followed those memories. He crawled over ten of the three-foot ceiling tiles before turning left and following the distant light. He knew the next quarter was over the drill site, and it would be lighted. When the light became brighter and he had crossed eighteen tiles, he pushed one of the tiles aside and dropped to the floor in the kitchen. By following the walls, he made it to the drill shaft area.

The backpack holding the containment core had been rigged from a rappelling harness, and Bryne fastened the ropes around the pole. He had to crawl on the floor and feel with his hands to find the drill shaft. He could hear hurried footsteps as he let himself into the shaft.

"Help me get them into the ruins," he prayed. "Take care of Rachel. Please let Rachel live. Take care of Melea. Get them home. See Mason home to his children." The prayer was a litany as he waited to hit the ground. He hit with enough force that his injured knee gave way. He fell onto the ruined streets of Babel. The pain in his leg and chest overwhelmed him for several moments. He was regaining his feet when hands grabbed him.

"I came to surrender," Bryne said. "You said you wanted me. I want to see again. Take me, and let the others leave."

"I think we all know that isn't an option, Bryne," said Carson's voice. "But we are glad to see you." He dragged Bryne across the main street of Babel with the strength of a young man. Bryne devoted all his strength to listening behind them. Before they reached the staircase to the cryogenic chamber, he knew there were four people in their group.

"I only have one question for you, Neill. Why was Babel destroyed?"

"We were not destroyed," Carson said. "The being who calls Himself, Yahweh, tried to destroy us because we would not serve him. He has failed. We will live again. We are gods. All the people will serve us this time." He shoved Bryne to the ground, and two men held his left arm against the floor. Bryne felt a knife scrape his forearm hard enough to draw blood.

"You will be inoculated," Carson intoned.

"God help me," Bryne said quietly. In that moment, he knew without doubt that God was listening to his plea. Strangely, he didn't feel alone in what he knew would be the last moment of his life on earth. At the same time, he had never wanted to live so much. He allowed himself to believe in eternity and said a prayer for forgiveness. His right hand felt the detonator in his pocket. "I love you, Rachel. If you can hear me, I know Jesus does love me."

"Your God can't help you," Neill said derisively. "He didn't save the people of Babel who worshipped Him. He will not save you. Babel will live again."

The prayer and Rachel's name gave Bryne the courage to activate the detonator. He expected to feel the explosion and then nothing more. Instead, he felt a faint thud against his back. Then, the light engulfing him made his limited vision disappear into whiteness. For a mercifully brief moment, he felt as if he were on fire. His awareness disappeared abruptly into the bright light.

Mason was able to activate the probe just before Bryne was thrown to the floor in the cryogenic chamber corridor. They saw him thrown down and saw Landers and Gibar restraining him. Rachel was weeping uncontrollably, and Melea was holding her with silent tears streaming down her face. They saw and heard Bryne say, "God, help me. I love you, Rachel. If you can hear me, I know Jesus does love me."

"He's lying on the core," Rachel said. "Please God. Please." She couldn't ask for what she wanted. What she wanted was the impossible.

"Your God can't help you," they heard Neill say. "He didn't save the people of Babel who worshipped Him. He will not save you. Babel will live again."

Rachel saw Bryne's hand press the button and felt as if she died inside. The light was blinding even on the computer screen. It engulfed Bryne and then filled the screen. The explosion obviously destroyed the probe. The screen went black before the station had stopped shuddering.

Mason closed his eyes and caught his breath in a sobbing gasp. "Help us, God. Help us to be strong." He called up the primary station screen and typed in the command for audio interface. It took his shaking hands three tries to enter the command.

"Computer, scan the station and ruins for any trace of virus Babel."

"This scan will take four hours," the computer said.

"Proceed," Mason said. "Also scan for humanoid life forms in Erebus station."

"There are four humanoid life forms in Erebus station," the computer said matter-of-factly.

All of them caught the significance of the number, but Rachel scrambled to the computer still praying for a miracle. "Computer, name the life forms in Erebus station."

"The life forms in Erebus station are Adams, Melea; Farmer, Mason; Madison, Rachel and McAllister, Bryne."

"He's alive," Rachel whispered. "He's alive, Mason. I'm going down there."

"Rachel, he can't have survived," Melea stammered. "He was on top of the bomb. If the others are dead, he can't be alive. Computer, report on condition of McAllister, Bryne."

"Life signs are detected," the computer said, "but ruins equipment has been damaged. Parameters on McAllister are unknown."

"I'm going down," Rachel said. "Even if he's dying, I don't want him to die alone."

She ran out of the generator room and to the storage rooms to get another rappelling vest and line. She was panting when she fastened the line. To her surprise, Melea appeared beside her and fastened her own line. Neither of them hesitated to enter the shaft. They were in the ruins in less than two minutes. It was almost warm in the ruins, forgiving them for forgetting their protective clothing. Melea broke open a light source and ran with Rachel to the building above the cryogenic chambers. Their descent was difficult because of debris. They passed incinerated ice mummies and on the stairway the desiccated flesh that had been Carson, Landers and Gibar. Rachel steeled herself for the worst. She was not prepared for what they found.

Bryne was lying on the shell of the containment core. He was unconscious, but his body showed no signs of having been atop the bomb. Rachel almost fell in her frantic attempt to reach him. His pulse was strong under her fingertips, but he made no response to their touches. Other than the deep scrape on his forearm, he showed no signs of new injuries. Despite being believers, they were shocked into silence.

Rachel and Melea carried Bryne back to the drill shaft between them, and Mason helped them hoist him out. With the last members of the team inside the dome, they sealed the drill shaft and returned to the laboratory.

CHAPTER 17

It was spring in Antarctica and November in Houston when the crawlers came to collect the remaining team. The storms kept them from coming until then. The crawlers carried away four people and hundreds of pounds of artifacts and computer data. The team was transported in an isolation chamber provided by ISC, and when they were at a safe distance an ultraviolet bomb was detonated just above the station. The isolation chamber was subjected to twelve days of scans before the team was released for debriefing and medical examinations.

Rachel was allowed in the room when Bryne's brain scan was being read. The neurologist defined the areas of damage. "His optic nerves were severely damaged by the laser. I don't know why he has light perception, but he won't ever have more than that. This form of blindness is untreatable. I'm sorry."

"We survived," Bryne said. "I can live with the consequences."

"I should congratulate you, Dr. McAllister," the doctor said. "You do know you were given a second Nobel Prize?"

"I've had a prize much greater than that one," Bryne said. He reached out for Rachel's hand, and she closed both her hands around his tightly. "Did you scan my DNA for any UV damage?"

"There's no signs of any damage other than the rib fractures, the cartilage tear in your knee, and the optic nerve injuries," the doctor said. "You all obviously shielded yourselves very well from the radiation."

He flipped through Rachel's chart. "No one shows any signs of radiation exposure which is fortunate because Dr. Madison is six weeks pregnant. I was worried about your exposure to the antiviral agents, but I see you've been off them for eight weeks."

"We ran out," Rachel said. "Fortunately our scans were negative for Virus Babel by that time."

"The embryo looks completely normal," the doctor reassured them. "You should still see your obstetrician as soon as possible. Dr. McAllister, you need to begin visual rehabilitation. Do you want to schedule that here or in England?"

"Let it begin here," Bryne said. "We've been doing some of it ourselves. It passed the time while we were waiting for rescue. If we start the formal training now, it will give us time to decide where we'll be living."

He held Rachel's arm as they left the examination room and walked just behind her as they returned to Melea and Mason. Mason was surrounded by his pregnant wife and extended family members. Mrs. Farmer came to embrace Bryne.

"Thank you," she said. "Thank you for bringing Mason home."

"Thank you for allowing him to come," Bryne said. "I'm sure we would have died if not for his talents. I'll make certain you get your stipend soon, Mason."

"Thank you, Bryne." Mason took Bryne's hand between his. "Thank you for everything. I'll let you know when we get our church."

"We would want to be there on the first Sunday," Bryne said. "We'll let you know where we end up."

Melea came to him when the Farmers left the room. She reached out to both of them, and Bryne embraced her as soon as her hand closed on his shoulder.

"Well, Mum, you're going to be a grand mum. We were thinking of naming a girl, Arielle, and a boy, Arthur." He put his hand on her face to feel her expression. Her smile was easy to discern. "You could come live with us."

"Maybe when the baby comes," Melea said. "I want to get back to the university for a few months and write up my data. You'll be in visual rehabilitation. If you invite me to Sweden, I won't say no. I'm thinking of applying for Neill's job, but don't let my decision sway you on your future home." She hugged Rachel. "Take care of him. Message me at least once a week. I love both of you."

"We love you," Rachel said. It was very quiet when the door closed behind Melea. Bryne put his hand on Rachel's abdomen gently and then pulled her close to kiss her belly.

"You said it was true," he said as she put her arms around him.

"How does it feel to know you're going to be a father?"

"When you told me, I could see tomorrow." Bryne spoke as if he could read her mind. "They said we could leave when they finished the medical clearances. I sent word to the university staff in London about my disability. They phoned while you were having your examination. They still want me. We just need to decide if we want them. Let's go to your apartment. We can call a taxi."

"I think Dad might be waiting for us," Rachel said. "They wouldn't let him see me until we were cleared."

"Do you suppose he'll refrain from revenge until I'm better able to defend myself?"

"You've survived worse." Rachel pushed him down into the closest chair and sat in his lap. "What did you tell them? About the explosion?"

"I didn't," Bryne said. "They'll want an explanation, and the one they'd get defies the laws of nature. I don't mind so much being disabled by blindness. Being confined to an asylum would be another matter. What did you tell them?"

"Nothing," she said, "but I feel guilty about that. I feel like we should tell everyone. If they don't believe, it's their loss." She kissed him and looked into his eyes, wishing he could see her and thanking God she could see him.

The knock broke them apart. "Who is it?" Rachel said.

"It's Dad, Rachel. May I come in?" They both stood to meet him.

The colonel had been ready to hate his son-in-law. He had wanted to annul the marriage if possible, but after viewing and hearing the Erebus station recordings, his feelings were no longer certain. The tapes had told him Bryne McAllister had offered his own life to save the rest of the team, including Rachel. It was a sacrifice that was difficult to ignore especially when the recording also carried Bryne's voice asking God for help.

As Andrew Madison crossed the room to meet his daughter and son-in-law, he realized there was something very different about the scientist. It was something much deeper than a physical change. McAllister looked physically like his father-in-law remembered him except for a full mustache and beard. There was something different in his face that Colonel Madison initially attributed to his loss of vision. Bryne's eyes stared straight ahead and reaffirmed that the scientist was blind.

The colonel ignored Bryne until he had embraced Rachel, holding her with all of his emotions displayed.

"Life isn't fair, but God has been more than kind in bringing you home," he said to his daughter.

"I'm sorry, Colonel," Bryne said. "I have to take responsibility for what happened. It was my project."

"There were unforeseen circumstances," the colonel said. "Sit down, Dr. McAllister. I've been asked to complete your debriefing for ISC."

Rachel guided Bryne back to the chair and sat beside him holding his hand. The colonel sat across from them.

"We've watched all the computer recordings. We've just started on the technological data. We were most interested in the recording of the solar bomb's detonation. Where was the bomb, Dr. McAllister?"

"It was in my rappelling equipment. I was wearing it on my back."

"You were wearing the bomb when it was detonated?" the colonel asked. "How did you survive?"

"I don't know," Bryne said slowly. "I just know I did survive. There's no scientific explanation. I should be dead. God must have spared my life despite the way I lived before I knew Him."

"We found Bryne next to the cryogenic chamber," Rachel said. "We wouldn't have looked, but the computer said he was alive. He was unconscious, and he didn't awaken for thirteen hours. The scans couldn't even find evidence of UV damage or burns. Everything and everyone around him was incinerated by UV radiation."

"What do you think happened, Dr. McAllister?" the colonel said.

"I think God let me live," Bryne said intently. "Probably no one else will believe me, but I don't care if I'm considered a daft fool. Only a miracle can explain how I came to be here." He smiled in

Rachel's direction as if he could see her. "Rachel was praying very hard for me. I was praying very hard for her. God answered our prayers. You can ask Melea and Mason."

"We did," the colonel said. "They told the same story. I didn't think you were the right man for my daughter, Dr. McAllister. When I'm wrong, I admit I'm wrong." He took Bryne's hand and shook it. "What you brought back will advance computer science by centuries. We're frankly amazed at how much research you were able to complete despite your injury."

"Dr. Adams and Rachel were very efficient," Bryne said. "I helped them as much as I could."

"We're very pleased with the results of your expedition, and you're going to be pleased with your compensation," the colonel said. "We will, of course, compensate the heirs of the other men. Outside of the viral infection that drove the others mad, I don't think we should release any information about their deaths."

"We'd like to put this behind us as well," Bryne said.

"Let me drive you to Rachel's apartment. We've stocked your refrigerator so you can just go home and rest."

"I don't think we've even thought about resting," Rachel said. "We just want to go walking in the sun before the winter comes."

It was a warm November day in Houston. They rented a car and drove out of the city to the beach at Galveston. They both took off their shoes and walked in the sand with Rachel guiding Bryne.

"You came to my favorite place in this part of the world," he said with the wind in his face. "Tell me what you see."

"I see you smiling," she said. "It's as bright as the sunshine."

"I'm thankful," he said. "I'll always be thankful for this day and every day we have together. As they walked along the water's edge beside an ocean Bryne would never see again, he and his wife knew their lives had never been more in focus. When they stopped at the edge of the ocean so Rachel could watch the sun set into the surf she asked him what he could see.

"Memories of seeing the ocean, but all I'm really seeing is what I need to keep my face in the light. If I keep my eyes turned to the light, I'll see what God wants me to see. With all the gifts he's given me, that's enough vision." And he believed it always would be.